A K.C. Flanagan, girl detective™ adventure

Mayhem on Maui

Collect all the <u>K.C. Flanagan, girl detective</u>™ stories!

**If you can't find the <u>K.C. Flanagan, girl detective</u>™ stories!
at your local bookstore:**

A. Complain (make it loud)
B. Place a special order
C. Order from an Internet bookstore
D. Order from the publisher (see order form at end of book)

Cataloguing in publication data

Murray, Susan, 1960-
(A K.C. Flanagan, girl detective adventure ; 3)
ISBN 1-55207-022-0
I. Davies, Robert, 1947-. II. Series: Murray, Susan, 1960- .K.C.
Flanagan, girl detective adventure ; 3. III. Title.

PZ7.M972Ma 1999   j813'.54   C99-940166-1

**Catch all the K.C. Flanagan news on the web at
http://www.rdpppub.com/KookCase**

Susan Murray & Robert Davies

Mayhem on Maui

ROBERT DAVIES MULTIMEDIA

ISBN 1-55207-022-0

Proofread by Maia Hébert-Davies

Ordering information:

USA/Canada:

General Distribution Services,
1-800-387-0141/387-0172(Canada)
1-800-805-1083(USA)
FREE FAX 1-800-481-6207
PUBNET 6307949
or from the publisher:

Robert Davies Multimedia Publishing Inc.
330-4999 St. Catherine St. West
Westmount, QC H3Z 1T3, Canada
☎ 514-481-2440 ▤ 514-481-9973
e-mail: rdppub@netcom.ca

The publisher wishes to thank
the Canada Council for the Arts,
the Department of Canadian Heritage,
and the Sodec (Québec) for their generous support
of its publishing program.

1

WELCOME TO LAHAINA

I find that the simplest moments of life are often the happiest. Don't you? For example, here I was, sitting under a sheltering, hundred-year-old Banyan tree in Lahaina town on Maui, Hawaii, with the woman I loved most in the whole wide world, my mom, Katrina Gigantes Flanagan. Side by side on the wooden bench, my head on her shoulder, we gazed peacefully upwards together, through the wondrous tangle of the huge tree's branches to where a flock of zebra doves cooed and burbled in the dappled sunlight.

"This place is just heaven, K.C.," Trina sighed, stretching her arms luxuriantly above her head, "Don't you love Maui?" (Just in case you're wondering, my older brother Rudy and I usually call our mother "Trina," which is what she prefers. We also call her "mother," now and again, and "mom" between ourselves.)

"Too true. Maui is great," I agreed. "Thanks again for inviting us along on the trip." When Trina and her fiancé,

Darrell Hughes, had generously offered to bring my older brother, Rudy, and me with them to the Hawaïan islands, naturally we had jumped at the chance. Mom nodded and gave me a sidelong, contented smile. She is brunette (like me!) and has the same green eyes. At that moment they were brimming with happiness.

"Well, angel, we thought you could use a break after all those awful things that happened to you in Mexico."

"Yeah, that wasn't much fun, that's for sure." I didn't really want to think about my recent experiences in Mexico right then and spoil the exquisite moment. Just the thought of my Mexican adventures was enough to make my blood run cold.

But mom wasn't quite finished.

"I know it was rough on you, K.C.," she added. "You had a terrible time in Mexico, but, believe me, when I say that nothing like that will happen here. You're safe with me. You're in paradise on Maui and I just want you to try to relax and enjoy yourself. All right?"

"All right, I'm relaxed. Can we talk about something else? Like, are you still looking forward to the gallery opening tomorrow night?" Phew! I changed the subject, getting onto mom's life, not mine. Trina nodded, flashing a grin which lit up her entire face.

"Yes and no. It's going to be a great success. I feel that. And I still can't believe I actually got Gerard to give me half of his art gallery for my sculpture exhibition. But you never know how the public will react. I just hope it goes well," she added, getting ruminative, a small frown marring her brow.

"It'll be fine, mother. Your stuff is way better than most of the work in the other galleries here, so you don't need to worry about that. At all." As I spoke, I gestured with my hand down the length of Front Street, the heart of Lahaina town. Lahaina is renowned for the prodigious number and quality of its art galleries and most of them were right in view, dotted along the waterfront.

Trina smiled at my lavish praise.

"You know, K.C., it's just a good thing you're not biased. Speaking of galleries, would you mind if we drop in on Gerard for a bit? I promise we won't stay long, I just want to make sure nothing was broken in shipping."

"Sure! Why not? Let's go."

It was a beautifully breezy day. The sun shone bright and warm overhead and Front Street stretched in all its charm before us. Down the block, a local with nine rainbow macaws had put up three, giant, paper, lacquered umbrellas, under which his entourage of large red, blue and yellow birds sheltered from the heat of the day. For a price, passing tourists could have photos taken posing with the multi-colored birds.

Our steps slowed as we approached and watched the birds' trainer deftly deposit a macaw upside down into the arms of a young woman and her husband. Smiling shyly at each other, the newlyweds locked lips for the camera while the three other macaws, perched on their shoulders, literally saluted the photographer, wings raised in a well-rehearsed pose.

Gerard's Gallery was on Front Street, sanwiched in between another gallery on its right side and an elegant restaurant on the left. Although the Gallery seemed small from the outside, once Trina and I went in, I could see that it was actually quite spacious. Lofty ceilings soared high overhead and white walls with discrete, brass, track lighting made the big rooms seem even more grand. They were designed to enhance the artwork on display rather than distract from it. Nice place for a show!

"Darling!" Gerard emerged from the back room to welcome us. I watched curiously as he warmly embraced Trina, who then turned to introduce me.

"Gerard, this is my daughter K.C.. K.C., meet Gerard. He's the owner of the gallery."

Gerard didn't offer to greet me with a hug the way he had my mother, but to be honest, I was a little relieved. We politely shook hands instead.

"A pleasure to meet you, Miss K.C." He winked at me in a friendly way and I smiled back. Gerard was wearing a black silk shirt and black linen pants with (I kid you not) blue suede shoes which exactly matched the color of his belt and the silk handkerchief peeking from his shirt pocket.

Just then there was a crash from the back of the Gallery. Gerard and Trina's faces whitened as they stared at each other in alarm.

"Archie?" Gerard's voice was slightly shrill. "Tell me that wasn't anything important! Archie?"

A man in a grey gabardine suit emerged from the back, grimacing and wiping his hands on a white silk handkerchief.

"Sorry, Ger. Didn't mean to scare you. That vase of flowers Mrs. Cunningham sent the other day fell."

"Oh, all right then. But let's replace the flowers for the opening tomorrow. She'll surely attend."

Both Gerard and Trina relaxed visibly.

"Nothing serious. Darling, shall we discuss the setup of the show? Let's look at what we've done here." Gerard escorted Trina back to the front of the gallery as he spoke.

"I put your work over in the main room, at center stage where it belongs." I watched as Archie glanced at his watch then went to unbolt the massive front doors, opening the gallery for business.

From around the corner came a cry of delight from my mom. "Gerard, it's excellent! I love the play of the light in here!"

I left Archie to his work, hurrying to catch up with my mother and Gerard.

Trina circled the room, pausing to examine one of her hand-blown glass creations residing on a pedestal in the front window.

My mother originally gained recognition as a sculptress through her work with stone, but about a year ago, on a whim, she had shifted from stone to the more fragile medium of glass. This was the first time the public would get a look at her new pieces.

The room was filled with glowing glass in all different shapes and sizes. There were colorful urns, perfume bottles, drinking glasses and plates, even a lamp shade in smoky violet glass flecked with what looked like drops of melted beads flung impressionistic-like across the surface.

I moved closer to the largest piece of all, an urn so large it was nearly my height. I studied it closely, fascinated by the shift and play of color deep inside the thick glass. Somehow Trina had managed to embed the glass through and through with flecks of what looked like gold leaf dust motes caught in a shaft of sunlight.

"This is absolutely gorgeous!" I said. Mom gave me a searching look.

"Do you really think so, K.C.?" For all her talent, Trina was remarkably insecure about her work, like most great artists. I knew from past experience that she wouldn't be truly satisfied until the opening of the exhibition, where she would witness for herself the pleasure her work gave others. And even then...

Gerard rubbed his hands together gleefully, including us both in a broad smile. "I anticipate a very successful opening night. The invitations went out weeks ago and simply *everyone who is anyone* is going to be here." Trina smiled back at him and was opening her mouth to say something, when our attention was caught by a Japanese woman on the street outside who walked past the Gallery window and paused, looking in at the urn.

She was beautiful in a doll-like fashion, stunningly dressed in a fuschia skirt and top which were stretched skintight across her body. As we watched, she gave her ultra-short skirt a quick, furtive tug downward, then turned to beckon someone to her side, pouting and pleading with him or her to come take a look at what she had spotted. Then she smiled sunnily, as a man stepped into view to join her.

He was Japanese, too, a heavy-set man wearing an elaborately-tailored silk suit in a rather aggressive shade of green. The couple made an interesting picture, framed by the window. Gerard, Trina and I watched quietly as the woman pointed to Trina's urn through the gallery window.

We couldn't hear what they were saying but an obvious argument ensued between them. She smiled and pleaded with him, gesturing toward the urn while he stood with his hands locked rigidly behind his back, giving no sign of agreement. She wore lots of bracelets and large earrings, a veritable walking jewellery store but I saw no engagement or wedding bands and so I deduced that she was his girlfriend rather than his wife.

Eventually, the Japanese woman put her hands on her hips, stomped one dainty foot and turned to march into the gallery, obviously intending to admire Trina's work with or without her recalcitrant escort. Trina and Gerard had just the time to exchange one surprised glance before the woman was inside, her heels rapping smartly on the black marble tiles underfoot.

Without speaking a word, she headed straight for the urn and stood before it, her face lit with admiration. Trina's smile took on an appreciative glow as she watched this reaction to her talents and Gerard stepped forward to officially greet the newcomer.

"It's lovely, isn't it?" He suggested, opening the conversation.

"Oh yes," the woman replied, "I simply adore it!" She made a moue of delight with fuschia-tinted lips (They matched her skirt, blouse, purse and red shoes).

"*Omae!*" Her gentleman friend had followed her inside the gallery somewhat impatiently. At his sharp command the woman snapped to attention.

"Yes, Hiroshi," she answered, her eyes meekly downcast. "Now isn't it even prettier up close? Don't you think it's pretty?"

Thus appeased, the man she had called Hiroshi strode forward, putting one foot before the other with self-conscious deliberation. His face wore a bored, impatient look and I had the distinct impression that he felt he had better things to do with his time than bicker with his girlfriend over a big piece of glass. A noncommittal shrug was as far as he was willing to go in his praise for the urn.

"It's all right. Now let's go."

"But Hiroshi-chan, I like this piece. I like it a lot. Darling, please?" There was a wheedling quality to her voice and as I watched she batted her eyes at him coyly. "For me?"

"The color is all wrong," he pointed out, peevishly. "It wouldn't match our carpeting at all. This vase is just too big and too red."

My opinion, which no one was asking for at the moment, was that, considering the awful suit he was wearing, Mr. Hiroshi had no call to comment on color. But I kept this thought to myself. Gerard shot Trina an alarmed glance and stepped forward into the awkward pause that followed Hiroshi's words.

"You're in luck, Sir, Madam," he said hastily. "The artist who has created this marvellous piece is right here." Gerard pointed to Trina and Hiroshi turned and stare slowly up and down at her in a way I, for one, didn't like.

"The exhibition is opening tomorrow night," Trina told Hiroshi politely. "You're welcome to come if you like." The young woman nodded and smiled but before she could accept Hiroshi held up a hand with a frown.

"*Jikan ga nai, yo*. We don't have time," he muttered, curtly. The young woman's smile became plaintive.

"But I want the vase," she repeated, gesturing toward the urn.

"It's an urn," I put in. The man she had called Hiroshi cast me a sour look.

"Urn, vase, what's the difference? It's the wrong color anyway." He turned to Trina with a calculating eye. "Unless maybe you can fix it for us?"

"Fix it?" Trina repeated slowly, puzzled. "I don't understand."

"Make it better," Hiroshi elaborated. "Put some, I don't know, put some yellow on it here, and here and here." As he spoke he wiped imaginary dabs of yellow across the glowing ruby red surface of the urn. I saw Trina shudder slightly as she grasped his meaning.

Gerard hastily jumped in, attempting to usher his contentious customers away from the urn toward a nearby bowl with a gold finish.

"Perhaps you'd be interested in another piece? This one maybe?"

"No," The young woman refused to be dissuaded from her choice. "This is the biggest one here. It's the one I want." She gazed up at Hiroshi beguilingly, peeking up at him from under what must have been false eyelashes. "Ple-e-e-ase 'Roshi?" she said in a weird attempt at enchantment. He seemed to reconsider (Does this kind of stuff actually work on men, I asked myself?), turning to Trina with a leer.

"OK. I'll buy the vase and throw in an extra, I don't know, hundred dollars over the price. You take it back to the shop and add more yellow for us. What do you say?"

Trina licked her open lips, aghast at his offer.

"Actually, sir, I think it's just fine the way it is," she replied, with a forced politeness.

"All right then, two hundred over the list price and you fix it for us." Hiroshi's eyes were narrowed with anticipation, clearly expecting Trina to jump at this 'generous' offer.

"Perhaps if you look around you'll find something else you like," Gerard quickly put in. "Ms. Flanagan is a very talented artist."

He waved at the room full of shimmering glass pieces but Hiroshi never took his eyes from my mother's face.

"I don't think so. Three hundred plus the asking price. That's more than it's worth."

The young woman looked eagerly at Trina, clearly hoping for her to agree, but I saw the ghost of a smile flicker in Trina's eyes as she waited a beat, then shook her head.

"Believe me, I do appreciate your interest in my work, but I cannot consider making any changes to this piece."

She looked Hiroshi right in the eyes as she said this and his mouth opened in an embarrassed half-smile. His eyes, which were rather small to begin with, nearly disappeared with his taut grin, and believe me, the effect was not at all appealing.

"Of course you can," he insisted unctuously. Now I must say, I was finding his manners strange, edging toward the repulsive. He hadn't even been interested in looking at the urn in the first place but now he was trying to bribe Trina to customize a work of art. I got the feeling that it wasn't the urn he wanted so much as it was the satisfaction of *buying* it, and buying the artist, if you know what I mean.

"Four hundred. My last offer." Hiroshi folded his arms across the solid expanse of his waistline and rocked back on his heels, savoring the moment. Mom's smile never faltered.

"Absolutely not. Perhaps you misunderstood. In fact, this piece is no longer for sale." There was now just a hint of brittleness in her tone, as though she'd suddenly had enough of the situation. "Gerard, dear, would you show me the rest of the gallery?"

Gerard acquiesced immediately, all smiles as he and Trina swept out of the room. I lingered long enough to see a dark look of frustrated rage replace Hiroshi's smile as he watched them go.

His girlfriend tugged nervously at her skirt and protested angrily, "But Hiroshi, I-want-the-vase!"

"It's too big and ugly anyway, Kimiko. And this was a stupid idea you had," Hiroshi snapped and then turned on his heel, heading for the door. After a moment the woman he had called Kimiko went tripping unhappily after him, footsteps echoing on the marble tiles.

I walked to the window of the gallery and watched as Kimiko ran down Front Street after Hiroshi, obviously nattering on about the urn. He tolerated her reproaches for only a moment then turned on her, jerking her arm roughly and snarling something in her ear as he pushed her ahead of him toward a long, red, town car parked by the curb three doors down.

Two men were at the limo, leaning over-casually against the hood, sporting dark sunglasses and matching dark blue suits with the jacket sleeves rolled up in a stab at jaunty fashion. One said something which made the other grin as they watched Hiroshi manhandle his girlfriend.

They stopped smiling and snapped to attention as Hiroshi and Kimiko reached the car. As the shorter one leaned forward to open the door, I noticed that Hiroshi got in first, without bothering to wait for Kimiko.

I watched until the town car disappeared down Front Street and then turned away from the window with a frown, and went to find Trina and Gerard.

2

AN EVENING IN PARADISE

Gerard and Trina had reached the back of the gallery by the time I caught up with them.

Gerard smiled weakly at Trina. "Sorry about that little ... disturbance," he was saying, raising his shoulders apologetically. She turned to give us both a long, intense look. At first, I was afraid mom was still really mad about the way Kimiko and Hiroshi had insulted her work but then she started to smile.

"Well *that* was certainly different," she murmured finally, her eyes crinkling into laughter as she shook her had. "Good Lord!"

She and Gerard stared at each other in mutual consternation.

"I thought I'd roll over and die when he asked you to 'fix' it for them! Can you imagine? What a moron," Gerard chuckled, obviously relieved that Trina had taken the whole thing as a joke.

"Yes, well," she replied, her eyes narrowing ever so slightly, "that was amusing in a way, wasn't it?"

I decided to offer my own opinion. "He was clearly a bonehead."

"I assure you he isn't a regular here," Gerard told us quickly, "although I'm sure I've seen him and his lady friend around town before."

"Hmmmmm," Trina murmured, idly fingering a packing crate in one corner of the room as she watched Archie deftly unpack the last few pieces of her work. Then she sighed and squared her shoulders, switching gears mentally.

"K.C., we should be heading back to the house if we want to make it in time to meet the boys." The 'boys' Trina referred to were her fiancé, Darrell, and my older brother, Rudy. We had plans to meet them in time for dinner Trina explained to Gerard as he accompanied us to the front door of the gallery.

"I'll see you tomorrow night, then and be sure to get here a little early, if you can," Gerard reminded my mother. "Don't worry about a thing, 'Trina. I just know the exhibition is going to be a huge success!"

"Thanks, Ger." Trina smiled and blew him a kiss, back to her normal cheerful self, now. My mother and I walked south along Front Street, past the banyan tree, the elementary school and the Lahaina Shores condominiums to the small house we had rented on the beach.

I guess at this point I should say something about Darrell Hughes, Trina's fiancé. He's a pretty shrewd Texas businessman. In the course of his ventures, Darrell has made himself a literal fortune in the oil fields and was easily able to afford the steep rental ticket on the house we were inhabiting on Maui for two weeks.

The beach house itself was unassuming, nestled behind a tall, stone wall which separated it from the road and surrounded by fragrant, white and lavender plumeria growing along the tall, privacy fence around the yard. Bypassing the front door, Trina and I went around to the back, and prepared to enter the house through sliding glass picture windows on the lanai.

"Hello? Darrell? Rudy? You guys home?"

There was no answer to Trina's words, so apparently we had made it back to the house first.

"I guess they're still out, K.C." Trina kicked off her shoes to step inside the house and I followed suit. The sliding doors opened onto the center of the house, a wide living room with a large screen television, a couch, and two wicker reclining chairs. A smallish kitchen adjoined the living room and down the hall from that was a master bedroom for mom and Darrell, and smaller rooms for Rudy and me.

Trina went to shower and change in her room. I loped out onto the beach with a book and a folding chair to sit in the shade of a mesquite tree near the water's edge. I stretched my feet into the surf, letting the ocean gently wash sand across my toes and as I did, my eyes fell on the long scar disfiguring my right thigh.

The scar was a memento of my encounter with a corrupt drug smuggler in Mexico and his nasty partners who had nearly been responsible for my death. It had been some months since I'd been instrumental in getting them all locked up in prison for good, but I was still getting used to the idea that I could sleep safely at night again.

In the weeks that had passed since my return from Mexico, I had done some serious soul-searching about my own natural compulsion to investigate things and had concluded that it wasn't necessary for me to solve every single mystery I came across. Nor was it my job to catch every single villain in the world. After all, there must be a limit to how much one single person could do!

In fact, I had finally realized that it would be far better for everyone concerned if I simply retired from detective work altogether. Here on vacation on Maui, I fully intended to practise this new philosophy, no matter what happened.

A flash of movement on the sand caught my eye. I glanced down in time to see a small sand crab pop out of its burrow and then cautiously and daintily pick its way across the beach. When I looked further, I noticed dozens of other sand crab burrows, ranging in size from tiny to fist-sized, peppering the sand of the beach along the shoreline.

"Hey K.C.!" I heard a shout and squinted at the silhouette of two men approaching. As one, the sand crabs all dashed for the safety of their burrows, leaving wispy tracks behind them as they fled from Darrell's and Rudy's approach.

"Is Trina back yet?" Darrell called.

I stood and picked up my folding chair, turning to greet the "menfolk."

Darrell is about six feet tall and dark-haired, with a muscular build. His eyes are very blue and steely, but he has a slow, sweet smile which can charm the coldest heart. He was turning it on me then and I smiled back like I was in a tractor beam as I fell into step with them.

"Snorkeling, huh?" I eyed the equipment they were carrying, "How was it?"

Rudy flicked a lock of long, wet, reddish-brown (he takes after our father) hair out of his eyes and grinned at me. "Great! It's shallow until a few hundred yards or so out from shore, then the bottom of the ocean floor just drops off and there are reefs and caves and stuff. We're going diving on Thursday, want to come?"

"Sure, sounds like fun." I followed Darrell and Rudy (their longer legs always give them a pace or two on me) as they entered the house though the sliding doors in back.

"Where did you get the snorkeling equipment, anyway? One of the rental places?" I was curious because along Front Street, there were a seemingly endless numbers of places renting equipment for snorkeling and diving.

"Well, actually, K.C., it was in the closet," Darrell shrugged. "Came with the house."

"Really?" A thought suddenly occurred to me. "What about the electric scooter in the garage?" I suggested casually, "Could a person maybe borrow that sometime too?"

Darrell winked at me by way of a reply, catching my meaning instantly. "Why, of course, K.C. darlin'. You just say the word and it's yours. Anything in the house. You know how to run a scooter?"

I grinned back at him. "No, but it looks pretty easy. Anyway, I already drove a golf cart in Mexico and—."

"Darrell, Rudy welcome back." Trina joined just then, coming from her room and hugging Darrell gently, while Rudy and I patiently waited out this display of affection.

Darrell is a tall man and makes Trina look like a china doll. Yet they still make quite a handsome couple, for all the disparity of their physical appearance.

Their personalities complement each other nicely, too. Trina is a little flighty sometimes but Darrell is as down-to-earth a person as I've ever known. He gives her rock-solid stability while she, in turn, shows him how to let go and have fun.

A few years ago I felt sorry when my parents split up,

but now that I'm older I see it was for the best. I must say, both Father and Linda, (Linda is Father's significant other), and Trina and Darrell are as happy together as anyone could hope them to be.

"How was your afternoon?" Trina asked.

"We went snorkeling," Rudy replied happily. "Met a nice girl on the beach, too. What was her name?"

He glanced at Darrell who raised an eyebrow at my mother, drawling, "Now, which girl would that be, Rudy? The one who put lotion on your back, the one with the poodle or the one on the Jetski?"

"Yes, they were all nice, weren't they?" Rudy remarked, dreamily.

Darrell continued with a wry smile. "Well now, they seemed to like you, too, son."

My brother has a few hobbies, you should know. Basically, they come down to sports, more sports, even more sports and girls, girls, girls. Up until a few months ago, he was dating an icky socialite named Pamela. In fact, she was a real twit, if you'll pardon my lack of female solidarity. I used to give Rudy an awfully hard time about Pamela this, Pamela that, but those days are, thankfully, over. Since breaking up with her, he has been playing the field. Good move, bro'! Last I counted, there were four ladies leaving messages for him on the answering machine at home.

Darrell stretched out on the huge wicker sofa at the end of the recreation room, patting the seat beside him enticingly. "Did you visit the Gallery?" Trina grimaced unbecomingly as she joined him.

"What was that for, hon'?" Darrell questioned the expression on her face. "You don't mind sittin' here next to l'il ol' me, do you?"

Trina flashed him an apologetic smile.

"Oh, sweetheart, it's not you! It was just that you mentioned the gallery and there was this, well, this person at the gallery, a Japanese man who wanted to buy my urn."

Darrell smiled at her. "But darlin', that's fantastic! Did you sell it to him?"

Mom met my eyes for a moment and we shook our heads at each other in shared amusement at the memory of the obnoxious Hiroshi. I mean, talk about a bull in a china shop!

"What's all this about?" Rudy interjected curiously.

I decided to explain. "This character called Hiroshi came into the gallery. Well, actually, his girlfriend came in first, but he followed and they decided they'd like to buy this beautiful urn that Trina created but only if it were a different color. So then, he tried to bribe Trina to change it. Can you believe it?"

Darrell's jaw tightened briefly and he gave Trina a sympathetic sidelong glance.

"It was a little annoying," she confessed. "I mean, it's one of my better pieces. I worked on it forever and he just ...walked right in off the street and told me to paint it yellow to match his carpeting." Trina's eyes narrowed at the memory. "It's hard not to take that sort of thing personally but after all, I was the one who wanted to get the public's feedback about my new work, didn't I?" She shrugged with a slightly self-mocking grin and added, "Serves me right, I guess."

"No it doesn't," Rudy contradicted her, settling into a wicker chair near the open doors. "That guy missed the point. I've seen the urn myself and I don't believe yellow would improve it at all. I think you've done it just exactly right."

Trina sent her son an appreciative glance as Darrell

said, "Sounds to me like as how he doesn't know much about art, this guy."

"How about you, K.C.?" Rudy looked expectantly at me and waited.

"What about me?" I replied, looking down at my toes and remembering my stay-out-of-trouble resolutions.

"What did you think?"

"About what, Rudy?" At this point, my brother gave me an annoyed glance and turned the volume down on the diving instruction video he had been watching.

"About the guy in the Gallery."

"What about him?"

"You there when this all happened, weren't you? What's your take on the whole thing?"

I paused, clearly remembering Kimiko, the flashy red town car and Hiroshi's two overdressed henchmen, then pushed the memory firmly out of my mind. "I don't really have much of an opinion, if that's what you mean," I told my brother a little untruthfully, "It's none of my business, anyway."

"You feeling all right K.C.?"

"I'm fine. Why?" Rudy still wasn't satisfied, and a slight frown played around his big brown eyes. "What?" I asked him eventually as he continued to watch me in silence.

"You're not acting at all like your usual Hawaii Five-0, double-O-Flanagan self," Rudy said. "The old K.C. we know and love would have had a theory about the guy in the gallery and would have shared it with anyone who'd listen. She probably would have even succeeded in lifting the guy's wallet to see where he lived."

I cocked my head a little considering his words then shook my head. "But that was then, and this is now." I brushed the hair out of my eyes and settled gingerly into the wicker chair facing Rudy. It was comfy, springy and soft. "And by the way, just so you know, I've decided to re-tire from detecting for good. The last six months have been, shall we say, a little *too* interesting for me."

"You've decided to give up detecting forever? Come on!"

"I have, indeed," I nodded with as much sincerity as I could muster. "It's way too much trouble. Detecting doesn't seem to leave any time to enjoy life. It's not for me."

"Ha!" Rudy didn't believe me for an instant.

"I'm serious."

"S-u-u-u-ure you are," he smiled.

"For real, *Rudolph,* so lay off," I insisted.

"Well, if you say so," he replied more indulgently, and we sat in silence for a moment longer, maybe just a bit on edge. I didn't care if Rudy didn't believe me about retiring from detective work. It was a moot point anyway. Trina was saying something about dinner and that brought me back from my thoughts. We spent the next few minutes debating our choice of food for the night. I suggested Japa-nese as a sort of joke about what had happened that after-noon at the gallery but, to my surprise, mom and Darrell nodded enthusiastically.

"Japanese food sounds good," Trina said, smiling broadly. "We haven't had sushi for ages and Gerard said that there are some great Japanese restaurants here in Lahaina."

"I could go for some sushi," Darrell said agreeably. "How about you, Rudy?"

Rudy shot him a wary glance. "Well, I—" he began, trying not to seem too disgusted by the idea of eating raw fish.

"Oh, come on, Rudy! It'll be good for you," I prompted

in a show of encouragement, "Fun, too. Maybe there'll even be karaoke."

"Karaoke?" Rudy repeated, puzzled by the word.

I explained cheerfully: "Karaoke is where they have that recorded background music and you choose a song to sing along with. Remember?"

My brother brightened somewhat at this suggestion. "Oh, of course."

Rudy has a delightful, booming baritone voice which he often exercises in the shower at home. In fact, lately, he has taken up playing the guitar (not in the shower, of course) and I think he has even been entertaining notions of starting a band. Personally, I'm guessing that this is because of the potential numbers of female groupies involved. Buy hey! Maybe his Irish musical genes are just rising to the top.

"OK. Japanese food might not be so bad, after all," Rudy answered quite seriously, jamming his battered, white panama hat (a souvenir from our recent trip to Cancún) firmly on his head as we followed Darrell and Trina out the door.

3

THE MURAYAMA SUSHI YA

Trina, Darrell, Rudy and I strolled down along Front Street, admiring the scenery. At six p.m., the sun was setting over the sea, silhouetting the island of Lanai, which lay across the water several miles to the southwest of Maui. In the far distance toward the west, I could even see the island of Molokai rising through the purple twilight haze.

Behind the banyan tree, along the waterfront was the Lahaina small boat harbor where row upon row of brightly painted pleasure boats were docked for the evening. Quiet tonight. But I knew that early the next morning tourists would be lined up, waiting to buy tickets for the all-day snorkeling and dive cruises which departed the Marina daily.

Not far from the Marina was the Carthaginian II, an old whaling ship which had been permanently docked and converted into a museum for tourists to board and study. It looked like a relic of another life which in a way I'm happy to say it was.

I had heard about the beautiful songs of humpback whales migrating off the coast of Maui in the wintertime and was glad that the whales had now become a tourist attraction rather than a target for the needle-sharp whaling harpoons which still adorned the deck of the Carthaginian II.

The waterfront was alive with people of all different nationalities. I knew that Maui was a popular destination for honeymooners and, indeed, they were not hard to spot. Here and there were quiet twosomes sitting on benches, fingers intertwined, as they looked dreamily out over the reflection of deep rose-reds and purples the setting sun left in its wake across the waves. A few months ago, such mush would have given me the shivers, but after I met the archaeologist, Julian Sayles, in Mexico, even if nothing ever happened between us, even if he was kind of a villain, I'm no longer so quick to judge other people's feelings.

We had chosen the Murayama Sushi Ya Japanese restaurant, down Lahainaluna Road and well back from Front Street. It was sheltered from traffic by a flaming, red stand of royal poinciana trees which bordered the entranceway. I looked around in wonder, feeling as though I'd stepped into another world, as I followed Darrell Trina and Rudy inside the restaurant.

The Murayama Sushi Ya was decorated like an indoor garden. The walls were paneled in an extraordinary light-colored wood on which were painted exquisitely executed watercolors of birds flitting through bamboo forests. There was a skylight overhead, hanging plants everywhere and a small, artificial stream winding through the room under two small, stone bridges.

The atmosphere was light and peaceful, enhanced by lilting shakuhachi, music barely audible above the gurgling tumble of a fountain in the center of the restaurant. A young girl in a red and white kimono greeted us inside the door with a smile and eyes cast modestly down toward the floor.

She bowed and indicated a row of assorted shoes parked near the door, evidently left behind by the restaurant's other patrons. "Your shoes, please."

We traded our shoes for slippers provided by the restaurant before following her any further inside, as is customary in Japan. After ascertaining that we wished a table for four, the girl in the kimono folded her hands in her lap and bowed slightly.

"This way, please." She led us towards a low table in the back of the room, near the fountain. "Please, be seated."

Kneeling, she distributed menus and helped us arrange ourselves on floor cushions called zabutons which substituted for chairs. I looked around curiously as we settled in. Our table was wide and long, and featured woven straw place mats and a small tray of assorted condiments in lacquered dishes which were labeled in Japanese.

Since Rudy and I (well, especially Rudy!) had little idea what to choose from the list of specialties the restaurant offered, Trina and Darrell ordered for all of us, selecting a variety of different foods from the menu — sushi, sashimi, maki-sushi, tempura. I was starting to salivate already.

"You're going to love this, Rudy!" Trina exclaimed. I hid a smile as he raised a dubious eyebrow at her enthusiasm.

Rudy agreed with formal politeness. "Sure I will, mom, sure I will."

Trina reassured him, saying, "Raw fish is nothing to worry about. It's as safe as any other form of meat, if it's prepared correctly."

"Oh?" Rudy repeated, "what do you mean 'if' it's prepared correctly?"

"Don't worry about a thing, bro'," I jumped in, patting him solicitously on the shoulder. "It isn't often at all that someone keels over dead after eating sashimi. Why heck, I think it's less than fifty deaths a year, all told. That's, why, let's see, that's only about four people a month, worldwide. Pretty good odds, eh, Rudy?"

"Gee, thanks for the good news, K.C." he replied, his voice heavy with sarcasm.

"Well K.C., of course that's mostly deaths from improperly prepared fugu, "Darrell put in seriously. Rudy shot him a worried glance.

"Fugu? What's 'fugu'?"

"Blowfish," I supplied cheerfully.

"Blowfish!?" Rudy shook his head, clearly aghast, "Isn't the blowfish a *poisonous* fish?"

"Why yes, but it's considered a great delicacy by the Japanese. They carefully remove the poison from the fish *before* they serve it, of course," Trina told him helpfully.

Rudy's eyes widened even more. "Did you, um, did you order any, mom? For us, I mean?" he asked nervously.

"No, not this time. Sorry, dear," Trina told Rudy regretfully, misunderstanding the reason behind his question. "But we can come back here some other night and try it then, if you like."

"Yeah, Rudy," I put in smoothly, "next time, right? I'll be sure to remind you."

"Sure," he replied, giving me a look of mingled amusement and annoyance. "Thanks K.C., I won't forget this"

"Ah, don't mention it. My pleasure." I waved his sarcastic gratitude away with a swirl of my hand. "Just doing what I can to help out."

"Mmm." Rudy's attention now turned to the series of black, lacquered trays which the waitress was bringing to our table. There were multiple dishes atop the trays, filled with pickled plums, salty miso soup, a kind of pickled radish called *daikon*, and, of course, raw fish.

Darrell and Trina had spared no expense. There was the sushi, a kind of raw fish prepared with rice and strips of algae, the sashimi, strips of plain raw fish, and the maki-sushi, exquisitely-made combinations of rice with things like soft-shell crab, cucumber, pickled, crunchy vegetables and other, unknown ingredients, rolled in algae strips and sliced. What a feast!

Rudy stabbed at his food, unsuccessfully trying to eat it with one chopstick until I showed him how to use them both. "Look, Rudy, pinch one between your thumb and your first two fingers, then pinch the other one between your last two fingers, squeeze, and *voilà!*" Here I gestured a little too energetically with the plum I was using to demonstrate my technique and it flew across my tray to land with a squishy thud near my pickled radish.

Rudy commented on this minor accident with relish. "Thanks for the tip, K.C.," he said, "Great technique. I especially liked that part at the end, there. Could you show me how to do that again?"

I was more successful with my second attempt and found the sashimi to be quite delicious. My favorite was tuna, my least favorite was octopus. A little too rubbery for my taste, personally.

We were all sitting there eating and quietly talking with each other, having a really pleasant meal, when loud voices from the entranceway interrupted our conversation, disturbing the peaceful stillness of the restaurant. The quiet

hush of voices around us turned to silence as six boisterous newcomers entered the restaurant, close on the heels
of the waitress in the red and white kimono.

Talking loudly, the group was seated about three tables
away from us and, to my dismay, I recognized Hiroshi,
Kimiko and the two Tom Cruise wannabes who had waited
for them by the town car outside the gallery. There was also
a thin white girl with them and a wiry, dark-haired man
who sat beside her. I recognized neither of them.

"Oh no," Trina mumbled, chagrined, "It's him, the jerk
from the gallery."

Darrell turned to follow her gaze and watched as
Hiroshi barked out his order for the entire party without
bothering to glance at the menu, dismissing the waitress
with an impolite little flick of his fingers.

"He's the one who wanted to buy the urn?" Darrell
asked. Trina nodded. We tried to ignore Hiroshi's presence
in the restaurant after that but it proved to be impossible.

A mere five minutes after their arrival he and his entourage had earned themselves the disapproving looks of
all the other patrons of the restaurant. The once-serene
atmosphere had been fatally disrupted by their presence
and I watched, hardly believing what I saw, as they ha-
rangued their waitress, sending back the four bottles of
sake they had ordered, claiming it wasn't hot enough.

The waitress bowed in silence and removed the tray
of sake bottles, disappearing into the back of the restaurant. A moment later, I saw a crew-cut Japanese boy about
Rudy's age emerge from behind the sushi counter and speak
with her in a low tone. It was clear to me that they were
discussing Hiroshi's table.

"Would you like to leave?" Darrell asked Trina consid-
erately.

She shook her head.

"I don't think so. I won't be chased out. Let's finish our food and then go on our own time." We went back to our meal but it wasn't possible for us to enjoy it in quite the same way. The sake disappeared rapidly across the room at Hiroshi's table, and the waitress was dispatched on a seemingly endless process of fetch and carry, heating and bringing more and more bottles of sake for her demanding customers.

The white girl kept her head down, saying little unless spoken to. She looked unkempt, wearing a black skirt and unpressed white blouse and I noticed that her nylons had a long run in the heel. She seemed sort of mousy, an unlikely member of the boisterous party. I found myself thinking that she was probably an employee of Hiroshi.

Kimiko had changed her clothes since we'd seen her last and was now wearing a black nylon dress with a long slit up one thigh. Whenever she thought Hiroshi wasn't paying attention, she flirted outrageously with one or the other of the two men with him, coyly pouring them more sake to drink when their glasses were empty and giggling a lot whenever they said something.

The small, wiry man kept his head down, concentrating on his food. I got the impression that he was more than a little embarrassed by the rude display his tablemates were putting on but as he couldn't do anything to stop them, he just tuned out.

At one point, Hiroshi looked up and spotted Trina, lifted his glass mockingly to her and spit out a toast in Japanese, saying something that caused the others at his table to burst into laughter. Darrell's fingers tightened and clenched into a fist but Trina shook her head at him saying, "Just let it go, darling."

Darrell shot her a smoky look, muttered something dour under his breath and continued to watch Hiroshi with barely concealed loathing.

"Hey, this stuff isn't so bad," Rudy remarked eventually, trying to change the subject. Having mastered his chopsticks to a fair degree he was wolfing his sushi down with cautious enthusiasm.

"Maybe we should order some fugu," I suggested with a straight face. When Rudy eyed me askance, I added, "For them I mean," gesturing to Hiroshi's table.

Before Rudy could reply, there was a crash from Hiroshi's table as one of his two underlings lurched heavily to his feet, his face contorted with anger, and shouted some obvious insult at the man beside him. It was apparent that the dispute arose from the fact that the object of his scorn had inadvertently spilled the contents of a bottle of sake all over the angry man's lap.

The man was livid, unleashing a torrent of furious Japanese at his erstwhile drinking buddy and although I didn't understand his words, they elicited gasps from the waitress. With a grim expression, the boy behind the sushi bar flung his spotless white apron aside and strode determinedly across the room toward Hiroshi's table.

He addressed Hiroshi with rigid formality. "I must ask you and your friends to please be quiet, sir. You are disturbing the other guests." There was utter silence at Hiroshi's table as his face turned a somewhat brighter shade of red.

He glowered at the boy, trying to look intimidating but succeeded only in looking as though the lights were too bright for him. "You don't want my business here? You dare tell me to be silent? Do you know who I am?" Hiroshi snarled.

The stoic boy gazed back at him, obviously fighting with

the urge to reply in Hiroshi's rude manner. "Please try to settle down, sir, or we will be forced to stop serving your table drinks," he finally insisted. I saw both of Hiroshi's buddies tense and scowl at the boy, their altercation over the spilled sake now forgotten.

"Yeah?" Hiroshi's eyes disappeared into the deep folds of his scowl, "Well maybe you'd just better—" His words suddenly trailed off and amazingly, his face turned an almost chalky white.

Fascinated by his sudden change in countenance, I followed Hiroshi's gaze to see what had startled him. But there was nothing across the room except a middle-aged, ordinary-looking Japanese man with pure white hair who was approaching from the back of the restaurant, perhaps summoned by the waitress. Hiroshi's blustering rage turned into a stony silence as the newcomer walked up to his table.

"So, Hiroshi Saito. It has been a long time. *Hisashiburi, ne?*" The white-haired man addressed Hiroshi quietly, taking up a stance slightly in front of the boy. He wasn't speaking forcefully. But by this time the little drama at table five had the undivided attention of everyone in the restaurant and his words carried clearly across the room.

"So, we meet again."

"Masataka Murayama, is that really you?" Hiroshi whispered, stunned.

4

BITTER ROOTS

* * *

<u>FLASHBACK</u>

Tokyo, Japan. Two young men, Hiroshi Saito and Masataka Murayama, are nervously conferring about their newest assignment.

"I'll keep an eye on the front door, you watch the back entrance, *wakaru?*" Hiroshi Saito is obviously the leader and he enjoys giving orders.

"*Hai, wakaru.* I'll watch the back door." Following instructions, Masataka Murayama creeps noiselessly away toward the back of the small hotel they are guarding while Hiroshi waits in the front of the building.

Hiroshi and Masataka have been given the task of guarding the hotel in which Hiroshi's uncle is playing mahjong with his buddies. It is an easy assignment, yet a fairly important one since the personal safety of four prominent Yakuza figures is at stake.

The Japanese mafia, or Yakuza as they are known, form an extensive network of underground crime throughout Tokyo and surrounding cities, controlling gambling and prostitution rings through-

out the country. Hiroshi Saito is the youngest son of Tadao Saito, a powerful Japanese mafia boss.

Despite Tadao Saito's high hopes for his only son, Hiroshi has yet to distinguish himself among his father's ranks. In fact, he has bungled two important assignments already and Tadao Saito has given the evening's task to Hiroshi and Masataka with certain misgivings, warning Hiroshi that if he makes any more mistakes he will be in serious trouble.

Hiroshi stifles a yawn and looks around sleepily. He spots a pretty girl hurrying home from her job at a nearby hotel and steps forward, blocking her way.

"Hello, beautiful. *Chotto matte, ne?*" he purrs smoothly, but she recoils from his advance. He follows her anyway, undeterred from his attempt to pick her up. Despite all experience to the contrary, Hiroshi fancies himself a ladies' man.

"Excuse me, please. *Sumimasen.*" Her voice is breathless and more than a little frightened, not surprising since Hiroshi has blocked her attempt to evade him. The late train to Shinjuku rushes through the foggy night close by, its lights illuminating the girl's scared face in a strange halo.

"Why are you in such a hurry? Don't you have time to talk for a while? Have some fun, maybe?" Hiroshi smiles persuasively at the girl but she shudders this time, stepping quickly away from his outstretched arm. Without a backward glance, she flees, past a street vendor selling roasted chestnuts from a wooden cart and into the fog, her footsteps fading in the night. Hiroshi watches her go in disgust, muttering something rude about females in general as he studies the starry sky.

Suddenly, there is the sharp sound of a gunshot, then, quickly, three more. Hiroshi freezes, panicking as he remembers that he was supposed to be guarding the front door of the hotel for his uncle. He turns and sprints the half block back to the hotel and sees that the front door to the hotel is now open, indicating that an intruder has entered through the front door. The door which he is supposed to be guarding.

Hiroshi is terrified. His hands shake as he fumbles for the gun in his pocket, dropping it twice as he enters the hotel. There is no sound from upstairs, where the mahjong game is taking place. Hiroshi tiptoes cautiously up the stairs and opens the door to his uncle's room.

An intruder, clad from head to toe in ninja-style black, is leaning over his uncle who is dead from a gunshot wound to the chest. His uncle's playing partners are also dead. As the intruder raises his gun and points it right at him, Hiroshi drops his own gun and begins to weep and beg for his life.

"No, please...please do not shoot me, I don't want to die."

The assassin scoops up hundreds of thousands of yen in cash as Hiroshi cowers passively before him, sobbing with terror and shame. It is at this point that Hiroshi's partner, Masataka Murayama, arrives from the back stairs, his gun in one hand and a grim look in his eyes. He quickly looks at Hiroshi and simultaneously fires off a shot, missing the assassin by a foot. The murderer shoots back at him, then in a flash, leaps out the window onto the thick red tile of the tiered roof.

Hiroshi babbles and murmurs in relief as the killer disappears. After one disgusted look at him, Masataka pursues the killer. But it is a futile chase. The killer is more familiar with the neighborhood than Masataka and, eventually, disappears in the narrow streets of the sleeping city.

When Masataka returns to the hotel, he sees that Hiroshi's father, Tadao Saito, has arrived on the scene with two bodyguards. Hiroshi, his senses now fully recovered, is telling his father his version of events and points at Masataka as he enters the room, blaming the mess on him.

"If Masataka had kept an eye on the front door like I ordered him to, none of this would have happened." The lie is brazen. Masataka is amazed by this outrage but doesn't dare protest. He knows better than to contradict the word of the son of Tokyo's biggest Yakuza Boss. To do so would be to openly shame Hiroshi in front of his peers, an act which would also shame Tadao Saito.

"Is this true, Masataka?" Tadao Saito asks and after a quick, wrathful look at Hiroshi, Masataka bows his head.

"If your son has told you this, then it must be true." he replies formally, glancing up to briefly meet Tadao Saito's eyes before looking down again. There is an expression of doubt in Tadao Saito's eyes as he looks from Masataka's bowed head to Hiroshi's flushed face. This is the first time that Masataka has made even the smallest mistake in his career with the Yakuza and Tadao is well aware of Hiroshi's track record of failure.

"I see," he replies thoughtfully. "Please leave us, Masataka." Casting one, surprised glance at Tadao, Masataka leaves the room. For a moment the room is silent. Then, Tadao Saito inclines his head at the door, indicating that his two bodyguards should also leave. Soon father and son are alone.

Hiroshi looks at the mahjong table, the dead players, his own uncle among them, and the open window. He looks anywhere and everywhere in order to avoid meeting his father's stare.

"Tell me again what happened," Tadao instructs his son firmly, crossing the room to put a gentle hand on his fallen brother's shoulder. There is deep sadness in his eyes as he listens to Hiroshi's halting narrative.

"I was guarding the back door and Masataka was supposed to be guarding the front door. I heard gunshots and when I came running up here, I saw the killer climbing out the window. Of course, I tried to shoot him but he was already gone."

"Where was Masataka during all this?" Tadao Saito asks quietly. He is standing by the window of the small room, the window through which the assassin fled. The window overlooks a narrow alleyway in the back of the hotel and Tadao can clearly see the door which Hiroshi claims to have been guarding while his uncle was shot.

"He was in the front of the hotel," Hiroshi's upper lip is beaded with sweat. "He must have wandered off and left the door open. Then maybe, after the shots, I guess, he must have tried to chase the assassin or something." In the alley below the window Tadao Saito can see the back door of the hotel. The area is clearly illuminated by a glowing neon light in the shape of a paper lantern, which casts a warm glow over the alley behind the hotel.

As he watches the back door swings out, opening to allow one of Tadao's bodyguards to exit the hotel. The bodyguard glances up and nods to Tadao, taking up a watchful stance near the door.

"Which way does the back door swing? In or out?" Tadao Saito asks Hiroshi quietly. Hiroshi licks his lips.

"That's a silly question, father. Why do you ask?" He is obviously stalling for time.

"In or out?" Tadao Saito's stare bores into Hiroshi , who gulps nervously then looks away, his eyes going suddenly shifty.

"Out, I think." Hiroshi says and when his father doesn't immediately confirm this guess Hiroshi adds hastily, "It's too dark in the alley, I could hardly see a thing and I didn't notice. The door might swing in, I suppose. Does it matter?" He shrugs and tries to smile.

Tadao Saito turns away from the window, his face a controlled blank. Hiroshi's comment about the alley being too dark to see has contradicted his statement that he was guarding the back door. Not knowing about the light of the neon lantern makes it obvious that Hiroshi has never been anywhere near the back door.

* * *

"It's been a long time, hasn't it," The white-haired man told Hiroshi pointedly and even from across the room I swear I could see Hiroshi sweating despite the air-conditioned coolness of the restaurant. The soft bamboo flute music in the background seemed suddenly spooky rather than soothing.

"Yes, a very long time." Hiroshi nodded jerkily in response, taking a deep breath while the man with the white hair exchanged a long glance with the boy. Not a single word was exchanged but a moment later the boy turned and stalked away from Hiroshi's table, his jaw set in a grim line.

The man bowed at Hiroshi, his eyes never leaving Hiroshi's and then he left too, returning to the back of the restaurant. Hiroshi appeared to be visibly shaken from this encounter, something which he tried to cover by pouring another round of sake.

The two men with him exchanged puzzled looks while the wiry man murmured something into the ear of the white girl, who nodded. After tossing his drink off in a gulp Hiroshi gradually regained something close to his normal color, but he was still obviously seriously unnerved by his encounter with the white-haired man. About four minutes later he abruptly tossed a wad of bills onto the table and got up to leave, earning surprised looks from the others at his table.

"*Ikou, yo.*" He addressed the rest of them quite churlishly and they all got to their feet, looking around the room half-sheepishly, half-belligerently. No one said a word as they left.

"What was that all about?" Trina turned to Darrell with a puzzled look.

"I don't know darlin'. Looks like your friend from the gallery didn't exactly like seein' that white-haired gentleman, whoever he was. Sure seemed scared of him, runnin' out of here like that." Darrell's eyes crinkled into a smile at the memory.

"What do you think, K.C.?" Rudy asked me quizzically.

I shrugged, thinking what to say. "Oh, I don't know." The situation was intriguing, fraught with overtones of history between Hiroshi and the white-haired man but as I had decided to MMOB (mind my own business) I had no desire whatsoever to get involved. The last time I had stuck my nose in to someone else's business I had ended up in some pretty hot water (well actually it was cold water to be accurate, but that's another story). Besides, I was retired from detecting. End of story.

"Come on, you can do better than that," Rudy teased me. "Calling K.C. Flanagan, Girl Detective, do you read me? Over."

"Give me a break." I was flattered by his words but protested anyway. "And besides, Rudy, you're the one who usually tells me NOT to get involved. So this time, thank you very much, I'm taking your advice." I waggled my fingers in a definitely 'hands off' fashion. "No involvement, no trouble. Nice peaceful vacation, see?"

Rudy gazed at me in genuine perplexity for a moment then shook his head. "You serious?"

"Sure am," I replied.

"Well good for you, K.C.," Darrell added heartily. "No sense in borrowing trouble."

"My point exactly." I nodded back, "I mean, think about it. All my detecting has ever gotten me is two ruined vacations and some really ugly nightmares. Believe me, they may say that crime doesn't pay, but in my case, detecting just doesn't pay."

"Are you still having nightmares, honey?" Trina sounded truly concerned. "I thought you told Gloria those had stopped." Gloria is the excellent shrink in Montreal who helped me get through my feelings about my awful experiences in Cancún. I shrugged, a trifle irritated with myself that I had mentioned my bad dreams to my mother.

"I haven't had one for a few weeks now, mom," I muttered finally as Trina continued to watch me.

"Well, K.C., if you need to talk to someone, remember that Gloria said you could call any time," she reminded me.

I just sighed. "I know, mother. I only mentioned the nightmares because I was talking about reasons why I plan to avoid trouble from now on. So please, you don't have to worry about me. I'm fine."

"Just so you know there are people who care about you, honey." My mother kissed me gently and dropped the subject. Trina is pretty cool about not nagging at Rudy and me but once or twice after that I caught her watching me when she thought I wasn't looking and I could tell that she was still concerned about me.

We went back to our meals after that and made small talk. This and that, odds and ends. There was some discussion of travel plans for the week ahead and more talk about Trina's exhibition the next day. Gradually the restaurant emptied out. Yet, Darrell, Trina, Rudy and I still lingered on, sipping green tea, listening to the fountain and generally just talking and relaxing.

The mood was abruptly ruined (second time that evening, now) by the sound of squealing tires and a crash from the street outside. The young sushi chef came running out from the kitchen to investigate, closely followed by the man with the white hair. As I looked up and across the room, I was just in time to see a bright flash of fire through the picture windows, near the front of the restaurant.

5

KENJI

Somewhat unnecessarily, Darrell shouted, "Get down!" What I mean is, we were already seated on zabutons, which is about as close to the floor as you can get. Nevertheless, we all bent over and waited for another attack on the restaurant.

"What the heck was *that*?" Darrell said, and standing up gingerly, he brushed himself off and carefully looked around. "You all wait here."

He went off to investigate the source of the flash, joining the sushi chef and the white-haired man who were, by now, near the front windows. Ignoring Darrell's advice, Rudy and Trina and I followed him and looked out the window as well.

There was a wooden bench on fire in front of the restaurant about two feet away from the picture windows. We hurried outside, where there was a strong smell of gasoline in the air, and I could see wh␣␣ appeared to be a whiskey bottle lying shattered on the pavement around the bench.

"Looks like someone threw a molotov cocktail at the restaurant," Darrell said, voicing my suspicions, as he held up one hand to shield his face from the hot blaze of the fire, "Somebody should call the fire department."

The young sushi chef ran into the restaurant to make the call while the rest of us stayed outside, watching the bench burn brightly.

"I don't get it," Rudy wondered, genuinely puzzled. "Why would anyone want to burn a bench?"

I cast him a reproachful glance and said, "Uh, Rudy—," but he continued, "I mean I know it's not the world's best looking bench but still you wouldn't think anyone would hate it enough to want to burn it, would you, K.C.?"

"Gee, Rudy, maybe they were aiming for the window but missed and hit the bench instead," I suggested with mild impatience, then watched as Rudy walked gingerly around the bench, leaning in close to study the wall next to the picture window.

"You know, K.C., I think you're on to something! I can see where the molotov cocktail bounced off the wall, there's a little patch of gasoline here. Whoever threw it didn't have very good aim, I guess."

A small crowd of passers-by had gathered outside the Murayama Sushi Ya by now and were standing around watching the action, snapping pictures of the flaming bench and whispering amongst themselves.

Two police cars careened onto the scene a few minutes later, followed by the town's local fire engine. The police took pictures of the charred bench and carted the pieces of the broken whiskey bottle away as evidence.

Darrell, Trina, Rudy and I all hung around to report

what we'd seen to the police officers. After all, we were eyewitnesses. The police interviewed us one by one to hear what we knew and take our statements. The white-haired man from the restaurant went first.

I saw Rudy walk up and say something to the sushi chef. They shook hands and Rudy began speaking in a low tone. By the time the last of the crime scene photos had been taken it was clear they had become fast friends.

Rudy brought the chef over and introduced us. "This is my sister, K.C. K.C., this is Kenji Murayama."

"Pleased to meet you," he said, very formally, shaking my hand and bowing at the same time.

"Likewise." I shook his hand and bowed back, studying Kenji as Rudy introduced him to Trina and Darrell. Like Rudy, Kenji was about five foot eight and muscular in an understated kind of way. He had deep, amber-brown eyes and straight, dark eyebrows; a serious kind of face.

"Thank you for taking the time to give so much information to the police. You have helped my father and me immensely," Kenji said. He then nodded at someone who was standing behind me and when I glanced over my shoulder, I saw that the white-haired man from the restaurant had joined us. Kenji smiled and introduced him to us.

"This is my father." Mr. Murayama was Kenji's height and resembled Kenji in looks except for the fact that his hair was pure white, instead of jet black like Kenji's.

He bowed formally to us all. "I must add my thanks to my son's," he said, "I am Masataka Murayama, and I own this restaurant. Please, may I offer you some tea? Or perhaps you would prefer sake?" Mr. Murayama's cordial invitation went in the direction of Darrell who smiled broadly and accepted for us all.

"I would be honored, sir," he said.

The waitress had, by now, left for the night, but Mr. Murayama was at home behind the counter, brewing us a pot of barley tea. He produced an Asahi beer for Darrell, and some delicious rice crackers for all of us to munch on as well.

"This sure has been one strange evening," Darrell remarked eventually, glancing sideways at Mr. Murayama as he toyed lightly with his bottle of beer.

Mr. Murayama's eyes narrowed, and he took a thoughtful pull from his own bottle of beer. "Yes, yes it has indeed been very strange."

"It was a good thing that the molotov cocktail didn't hit the window of your restaurant," Darrell observed, after a moment more.

"A good thing, yes," Mr. Murayama replied. His expression though was strangely bland.

"I wonder if this has anything to do with all the other recent fires in town." Kenji mused.

Rudy leaned forward with interest. "What other fires?"

"There have been two suspicious fires in Lahaina in the last week," Kenji replied, "I heard a rumor that there's some kind of a gang war happening on Maui."

"Rumors are everywhere, like unwelcome guests," Mr. Murayama said quietly. "They are of no importance."

"But it's true," Kenji protested, his eyes flashing. "A danceteria and a mahjong parlor have already burned down. And now they attack our restaurant too!"

"Kenji," Mr. Murayama didn't raise his voice but Kenji stopped speaking immediately. "I know you are upset after what has happened tonight, but you must learn to control your fear. Do not let it control you."

Kenji gave his father an annoyed look and subsided into silence, but his eyes spoke volumes.

Darrell gave Mr. Murayama a knowing glance and leaned back in his chair, draping an arm lightly around Trina's shoulders. She smiled and cuddled against him gratefully.

"So, dear friends, how long do you visit Lahaina?" Mr. Murayama directed this question politely to Darrell, obviously trying to change the subject. Darrell paused for a bit, then shifted into conversational mode.

"Well sir, we're rentin' a house on the beach for two weeks. Trina, here, is havin' an exhibition of her work at Gerard's Gallery, down the street." Darrell gave mom a proud nod. "She's really somethin' else. You should come by and see some of her stuff."

"You are an artist?" Mr. Murayama asked, as he studied Trina keenly. "What medium do you work in?"

"Stone usually, but I've been experimenting in glass lately. That's what's showing at Gerard's, my new line."

"You are interested in sculpture?" Mr. Murayama studied my Mother with new interest. At her nod, he continued, "Then perhaps you might like to see my garden." He rose to his feet with a smile. "Come, it is just outside." Trina flashed a grin at Darrell, got to her feet, and followed Mr. Murayama through a door in the back of the restaurant. After a moment, Rudy, Kenji, Darrell and I got up and went after them.

"My father works with bonsai trees," Kenji explained, a touch of pride in his voice. "He has quite a large collection."

When we reached the garden I was entranced to find myself standing among dozens of tiny potted pine trees, one foot tall miniatures of full grown trees. Along with the trees, several pony-sized boulders and a small, winding stream gave Mr. Murayama's garden the illusion of a being a forested mountain top.

"Bonsai is a kind of Japanese tree sculpture," Mr. Murayama told Trina who was stooping over one tiny tree, growing in a deep blue enamel pot. "We wrap the trees with wire when they are seedlings, so that we can bend and shape them. With careful pruning we are able to keep them small."

"These are fantastic. You must have devoted years to this."

At Trina's compliment Mr. Murayama's eyes grew distant. "I have worked with Bonsai ever since I came to Maui."

"When did you move to Maui?" Trina asked him politely.

Mr. Murayama shrugged, elaborately. "I was originally born in Tokyo, but came to Hawaii as a young man." His eyes crinkled in a sudden smile. "Very long time ago. Right, Kenji?" Kenji shrugged, then grinned back reluctantly as his father continued more seriously. "Kenji's mother died when he was very little and the two of us have lived here in Lahaina since then."

"Maui is quite the place to live, no doubt about it," Darrell nodded agreeably. We all stood there in silence for a moment, listening to the burbling splash of the stream running through Mr. Murayama's garden.

"Well," Darrell said finally, "it's gettin' late and we've had quite an evenin'."

"Yes, we should be going," Trina agreed. "Thank you for the tea, Mr. Murayama."

"Kenji and I thank you for your support this evening," Mr. Murayama responded sincerely.

"See you tomorrow, then," Kenji told Rudy. "You too, if you like, K.C.," he added for my benefit.

I raised my eyebrows, surprised. "Oh? What's this?"

"We're driving to Hana tomorrow," Rudy explained. "I

told Kenji that you and I were talking about going there and he said we could go with him. Isn't that cool?"

"You see, I have to drive to Hana tomorrow to take a computer to the new restaurant we're opening there," Kenji explained. "Rudy is definitely my guest, K.C., and I would be honored if you came along too."

I accepted quickly. "I'd love to go, Kenji, that sounds like fun."

"We're leaving at six a.m.," Rudy said, then grinned at my look of shock and added, "Just kidding, Kook Case. We won't be leaving until around ten in the morning."

"Thanks a lot, *Trudy*." I muttered. Rudy knows that I am not a morning person and teasing me about it amuses him no end.

We said goodbye to the Murayamas and left the Sushi Ya, returning to our house in a taxi which Darrell flagged down on Front Street. It was only a short walk home but we were all feeling tired and a little jumpy from our unexpectedly exciting evening, so a walk home in the darkness had little appeal. On the ride home, though, an odd thought occurred to me.

"Hey, you know what?"

"What, honey?" Trina asked.

"All the other times this sort of stuff happening on our vacations was always my fault somehow, you know?"

Rudy nodded, remembering. "The murder you witnessed in Puerto Vallarta."

"And the treasure thieves in Cancún," Darrell added.

I went on, "But this time you were all there. Right? You saw how it happened. It's not like I went looking for trouble, is it?"

"That's sure true," Darrell allowed thoughtfully.

"But anyway, in case you're all worried about what's

happened, I just want you all to know that I really mean it when I tell you I'm staying out of things this time," I told them firmly. "We're all here to have a nice, peaceful vacation and that's exactly what we're going to have."

The taxi pulled up at the house and we climbed out as Darrell over-tipped the driver and sent him off grinning from ear to ear. Darrell does that a lot, just because he can, I guess.

"Aren't you even a little bit interested in finding out what's going on?" Rudy asked me curiously as we entered the house.

"Not really, no." I wanted to be true to my resolutions of non-involvement. My mystery-solving obsession had maxed out, like I said. All it had ever gotten me was two ruined vacations, a scar and a bunch of nightmares. Well, maybe a few friendships too, but that was beside the point.

"Oh come on, K.C.." Rudy was regarding me with the look of one waiting for the other shoe to drop. When I said nothing more he frowned, "So that's it? That's all you have to say?"

"You betcha. That's all."

"You don't mean to tell me you're actually *serious* about giving up detecting?" Rudy persisted, a note of disbelief in his voice.

"I am," I nodded. I needed to be quite firm here.

"For real?"

"For real."

"I can't believe you're being this way!"

Rudy was thoroughly annoyed.

I felt my jaw drop in surprise. "Me?!" I didn't mean to sound shrill but pure amazement has a way of doing that to me. "I'm just trying to avoid trouble for once. I would think you'd be *with* me on this one, after all the other times you've told me to stay out of trouble!"

Rudy dropped onto the sofa and reached for the remote control, surfing the satellite signal for just the right sports channel. "This time things are completely different, K.C.," he told me coolly. "I would think you'd see that."

I kicked off my sandals and sank onto the sofa beside him. "Oh yeah? How are they different?" I asked.

"It's different because this time we're involved. We were right there when this thing happened. We can't *not* get involved!" Rudy insisted passionately.

"Ha," I replied sarcastically, "just listen to you."

"'Ha' what?" he retorted, incensed. "You mean you're just going to stand back and let the Murayamas try and handle this problem by themselves?" He stared me with his Agent Mulder look of exaggerated disbelief then demanded, "What galaxy are you from, alien. And what have you done with my sister?"

I decided to ignore Rudy's completely emotional male outburst by calmly fixing my gaze on the television, which was tuned to a channel featuring (for some strange reason) NBA dream team stars involved in world championship mud wrestling. But enough was enough. "Give me that clicker!" I barked, and snatched the remote control from Rudy's hand. A few nimble-fingered clicks later I found a quiet documentary featuring Hawaii's underwater world. After that I kept the remote on the table near me, far out of my brother's reach.

"I bet you'll change your mind anyway," Rudy told me after a moment.

"Will not."

"Will too," he replied smugly, "I know you, K.C. Flanagan. You'll never be able to resist getting involved in a mystery like this." I ignored Rudy's remark, watching as the silent beauty of the coral reef unfolded on the television screen before me.

"I sure got the feelin' there was more to the story than Mr. Murayama was tellin' us," Darrell observed after a while.

Rudy agreed. "He really didn't want to talk about the molotov cocktail at all, did he?"

"Odd how he shushed Kenji like that, when Kenji was talking about the other fires on Maui recently," Trina put in. "What did Kenji say had been burned down so far?"

"A danceteria and a mahjong parlor," Rudy supplied, "but the real question is who tried to burn down the Murayama's restaurant. Right, K.C.?" He waited, expectantly.

"Whatever the problem is, the police know everything we know, probably more, and they'll do the best job anyone can possibly do of following up on our leads," I told the three of them firmly, getting to my feet. "It's quite out of the question for any of us to get involved in this. And not a good idea, either."

They gaped at me in utter disbelief as I added, "I'm sleepy mom, so, good night all," and left the room.

"What's with her?" I heard Rudy mutter behind me but I kept on walking down the hallway to the privacy of my own room.

There was no way I wanted to get mixed up with a bunch of stupid people throwing molotov cocktails. Someone was bound to get hurt and this time, I sure didn't want it to be me. As I got ready for bed my right leg ached sharply, a reminder of my close encounter with disaster in Cancún a few months earlier. The brief spasm of pain helped strengthen my resolve to remain a bystander to the Murayama's drama.

True, the old, young and foolish K.C. Flanagan might

have rushed in and gotten mixed up in a big old ugly mess of attempted arson but the new and more mature K.C. knew better than to do anything so silly. Content with my grown-up decision, I read a few pages of a neat book on Hawaiian birds, then fell into a deep, restful sleep that lasted until the early morning light.

6

HIGHWAY TO HANA

Or rather, until the nine thirty a.m. light, as it turned out. I must have hit the snooze button one too many times, because when I finally emerged from slumberland, Rudy was knocking loudly on the door to my room.

"K.C., open the door! It's time to get up. Kenji will be here soon. Move it!"

(I lied, from under the pillow,) "Stop making such a racket, I'm awake already. Cripes!"

There was a short silence, then my brother contradicted me briskly. "No, you're not," he replied, "I bet you're not even out of bed. Now come on! Kenji's going to be here in a little while. Open the door."

"All right, for Pete's sake," I rolled over and groaned, opening my eyes, "Take a break, bro'! I'm up, I tell you."

"Then open the door."

Still wrapped tightly in the blankets, I wanted to stay in my little cocoon as long as possible, without giving Rudy an inch of satisfaction. "Like I said, Rudy, I'm up. You know, as in opposite of down."

"Then prove it and open the door, I want to give you your morning hug," Rudy repeated patiently. "I know you, K.C., you'll just go right back to sleep the minute I stop talking to you."

Finally, I got up, padded to the door, unlocked it and swung it open, squinting all the while. "That's not true," I squeaked up at him, "See? I'm wide awake."

"And looking like a little ray of sunshine too," Rudy grinned down at me, "Now hustle up. You've got fifteen minutes until Kenji gets here. There's tea and toast for breakfast in the kitchen."

"I'm hurrying! I'm hurrying!" I sighed and closed the door, trying to unscramble the cobwebs. I'm just not a morning person. Any of you gals out there like me, raise your hands. Ha! Just as I thought. We're in the majority.

The day ahead called for a lightweight pair of khaki pants and a long-sleeved white blouse, along with my wide-brimmed straw hat, of course. Maui boasts perpetually beautiful weather. The U.V. index is always high, and I knew that an hour's direct exposure to the Hawaiian sun would be more than enough to burn my skin to a crisp.

When I reached the kitchen I disocvered that Trina and Darrell had already gone. Trina had left a quick note to let me know that she and Darrell would meet us at the house later that evening before the exhibition and to remind us both to be on time.

I munched down three pieces of toast with jam before Kenji arrived and joined Rudy and me for coffee. The guys sat outside on the lanai talking about events of the night before while I finished my breakfast. I couldn't help overhearing their conversation but tried not to pay attention, in accordance with my new-found resolve to stay detached from detective work.

All the same, I heard Kenji tell Rudy that his father had completely refused to talk about the entire business of what seemed more and more like a failed attempt to burn down the Murayama Sushi Ya. Not only that, but when Kenji had expressed a desire to get to the bottom of things, Mr. Murayama had strongly suggested to his son to lay off and let the police handle things. Sound parental reasoning, smarter to be followed, I nodded to myself maturely.

"So did you talk to the police?" Rudy asked.

"Of course," Kenji replied, "but they wouldn't tell me very much. They're assuming it has something to do with the other fires they've been investigating on Maui lately but they don't have any idea who the firebug is." I got up and stacked my dishes carefully in the sink, missing out on the rest of Kenji's words. By the time I rejoined them, the conversation had shifted to the topic of the trip to Hana.

"You guys ready?"

At our nods Kenji continued, "Good! Let's go." Rudy and I followed him outside and I was intrigued to see that Kenji was driving a silvery green Jeep Wrangler, a compact but powerful open vehicle capable of going almost anywhere.

"What? Are we going cross-country?" Rudy joked as he started to climb into the front seat beside Kenji.

"Hey! 'Ladies first', or haven't you heard, Rudolph," I said quickly and blocked his access with my leg.

"OK, KookCase, you want the 'suicide seat, be my guest," Rudy answered with a smirk, making a grand gesture of helping me into the front seat and helping me buckle up. "You take care of the precious front cargo, Kenji. I'll ride shotgun on the hardware in the back," he added, speaking right over my head to our friend. Sheesh!

Kenji jumped in with a question of his own and a wicked smile. "Haven't you heard about the road to Hana?"

"What about the road to Hana?" I asked, as Rudy buckled himself in behind us, wiggling to get comfy with the cardboard boxes containing various computer components.

"It's sort of, well let's say it's a little winding," Kenji answered. "Are either of you afraid of heights?"

Rudy shook his head. "Nope."

"Not me." I assured Kenji.

He nodded and said, "Good."

Without explaining that last remark, Kenji took Highway 30 south out of Lahaina, following this coastal road until it veered inland.

As he drove, Kenji told us a little about the island. Maui is the second largest of the eight Hawaiian islands which were originally formed many millions of years ago by hot magma from the earth's core flowing up from a crack in the floor of the sea.

According to traditional Hawaiian storytelling chants however, the Hawaiian islands were born in an entirely different fashion. They were fished up from the ocean floor by a demigod by the name of Maui. Revered throughout the Polynesian islands, Maui was said to be a half human, half mythological sorcerer/prankster who served his people well with his remarkable feats and adventures.

Maui procured fire for mankind, lifted up the sky so humans could walk upright on the islands and lassoed the sun god himself with a braided rope made from human hair so that the days could be longer. This he did from the top of Mt. Haleakala, literally translated as 'house of the sun'.

Since the island of Maui had the distinction of being the only one of the Hawaiian islands to be named after a god, the official island theme was 'Maui no ka oi!', which means 'Maui is the best'!

Kenji told us some other pretty interesting things about some of the other natural phenomena of the islands, such as earthquakes, tsunamis, hurricanes and such which were not at all part of the Flanagan family's everyday life at home in Montreal.

It made me shiver to hear him describe the evacuation drills which residents along the coast of the island practiced so that they would know how to leave their houses in a hurry if a tidal wave came roaring toward Maui in the middle of the night. I had to conclude that even paradise had a downside.

"What's growing in all these fields?" I asked Kenji. We were driving across the isthmus connecting Mt. Haleakala to the West Maui mountains and on the flatlands all around were fields filled with a profusion of plants with sharp flat green leaves growing about five feet high.

"Sugarcane," Kenji replied.

I squinted out at the far side of the field, noticing that a thick yellowish cloud of smoke was rising from the edges of the field. The smoke itself smelled slightly sweet, like caramel. "Hey! The field is on fire!" I told Kenji excitedly, "Do the farmers know it's burning?"

Kenji smiled at my concern. "That's how they harvest sugarcane on the island. They grow the sugarcane plant until it reaches maturity at about twenty-two months. That's when the leaves on the stalks are all dried and dead and can be burned off."

"Why would anyone do that?" I wanted to know, "Doesn't burning the sugarcane ruin the sugar?"

Kenji shook his head. "No, K.C. When the leaves are all burned off the sugarcane is easier for the farmer to harvest and carry. Also, the heat from the fire crystallizes the sugar inside the cane. That way, it's much lighter to carry and easier to process. Chinese immigrants to Hawaii brought the sugarcane harvesting technology with them many years ago. For a long time, sugar cane was a major industry of Maui."

Out of curiosity, I decided to prod Kenji a little. "Well, so what's the major industry now?" Kenji smiled enigmatically in response. "Officially, it is definitely tourism. We also grow pineapples here and on the island of Lanai, but that industry has fallen off lately. Unofficially, you know, there's something called 'Maui Wowee.' But it's not exactly described on the tourism brochures, and the producers will never talk to you about it. After all, it's not entirely legal. In fact, it isn't legal at all" That got me thinking!

After a fifteen-minute drive from Lahaina we reached the town of Wailuku near the northern coast of the island where Kenji stopped to fill up on gas. I wandered inside the small mini-mart attached to the gas stand and picked out a couple of bags of chips and assorted juices. A brightly colored tee-shirt caught my eye. It featured a frightened-looking tourist with big round eyes at the wheel of a car on a very narrow, very winding road along a mountainside. "I survived the road to Hana!!!" proclaimed the bright red letters on the shirt.

I paid for the snacks and rejoined the guys in silence. Once we were back on the road again I found the section in my guide book pertaining to the town of Hana and the road which led there. "Kenji?" I turned and gave a sweet smile to our new friend.

"Yes K.C.?"

He grinned as he met my eyes briefly and I realized that he must have been watching me reading about Hana.

"What's this about the road to Hana being," I quoted from the guide book, "'a narrow, two-lane road consisting of hairpin turns with a drop of hundreds of feet to the water below'?"

"Ah, that's just tourist stuff, K.C. Still, let me put it this way, the four wheel drive on our Jeep will probably come in handy."

"What do mean by 'come in handy,' Kenji?"

"It's a really cool drive, if you know where you're going," Kenji continued reassuringly. "The only really dangerous section of the road around the island is past the town of Hana, where the road turns into a single lane. Most car rental companies don't insure their cars for that stretch of road, it's too hazardous."

Rudy woke up from his daydream and gave Kenji a skeptical look. "But you've driven it. Right, man?"

"Sure, Rudy. Once or twice, at least," Kenji admitted, "but we won't be driving all the way around the island today. We'll just be going to Hana and back."

We had now reached the first of a long, low series of curves along the hillside and the ocean was becoming visible through the trees. Kenji shifted the Jeep into a lower gear and surged up the incline, passing a tour bus filled with tourists parked by the side of the road.

As we passed through a series of small foothills Kenji pointed out groves of mango trees, kukui nut trees, and koa trees. I listened with interest as Kenji explained how the ancient islanders had preferred the wood of the Koa tree for use in building the hollow, dugout canoes they used to paddle around the islands.

Farther along the road there were weird-looking gaping holes in the cliff every fifty feet or so along the side of the road which Kenji said were volcanic vents. "The mountain itself is honeycombed with lava tubes," Kenji explained. "There are tons of volcanic caves like these, some even large enough for exploring."

I shuddered slightly at his words, remembering the last time I had gone exploring in a cave in Mexico. I didn't think I was ready for any more underground exploring just yet.

"So we're actually driving across a big old volcano?" Rudy asked curiously.

Kenji nodded. "That's right. Mt. Haleakala rises thirty thousand feet upward from the floor of the ocean, which makes it one of the tallest mountains anywhere on earth, by the way."

"But it's a dormant volcano though, right?" Rudy asked.

Kenji replied with a smile. "Sure, for now, anyway. But who can know the future?" he told us. Rudy and I exchanged uneasy glances but Kenji drove serenely onward. "The road gets a little steeper here," he informed us unnecessarily, as the vehicle's hood had by now risen to a steep angle and was almost in our faces.

To the right of the vehicle I could see a sheer wall of lush green growth, and to the left side was a sharp drop downwards to the ocean. It was a little alarming at first but after a while I decided to trust in fate, leaned back in the seat and enjoyed the view, which was breathtaking.

I looked out of the Jeep to my left, staring across miles of ocean reflecting the blinding sun, and every once in a while when I looked to my right I could see an occasional sparkling waterfall as it cascaded down the mountainside through the trees, creating little rainbows that glittered and danced in the sunshine.

I saw what looked like an aqueduct, a shallow concrete waterway running parallel to the road through the trees. When I asked Kenji about it he explained that a series of catchments, or stone waterways, had been built all through the mountainous rain forest and that the water collected by these was being used to irrigate surrounding farms in the lowlands.

Cattle ranching was a also major industry on Maui, Kenji now added. Most of the southwest side of Mt. Haleakala was given over to grazing pasture for the numerous herds of dairy cattle which were farmed there.

Traffic on the Hana highway was fairly brisk and heavy but nothing moved terribly fast. There were numerous tour buses to be seen, and many tourists in rental cars stopped here and there by the roadside to photograph the waterfalls and each other against the stunning backdrop of the ocean vista and lush mountain forests.

We reached Hana around noon, judging by my tummy clock which had begun to grumble, arriving in the small town in time for lunch. Phew! Because of the winding road it had taken us two full hours to drive less than fifty miles.

"We'll just drop this off and grab a bite to eat here, then head back. Or we could look around some, if you like. There's a really cool series of waterfalls at a place called O'heo Gulch just up the road," Kenji said, as we pulled into a small parking lot down the street from a local landmark called the Hasegawa General Store and parked the Jeep. I got out, stretched my cramped-up legs and studied the new restaurant building.

The Murayama Sushi Ya in Hana was smaller than the one in Lahaina and was a smooth, if odd blend of eastern and western architectural styles. It was a white clapboard building topped by a Japanese-style red tiled roof and wrapped all around by a wide-screened veranda with outdoor seating for customers.

We climbed a short flight of stairs up to the veranda

where I studied the discreet sign by the door which listed the menu choices and prices. Kenji knocked on the door but we waited in vain for a response. After knocking a few more times Kenji finally shrugged, opened the door, and walked in. Rudy and I followed, each of us carrying one of the cardboard computer boxes.

Kenji shouted, "Hide!" (it sounded like 'hee day') and we heard footsteps from the back of the restaurant. A short, middle-aged Japanese man hurried out to meet us, smiling when he saw what we had brought for him.

"Kenji, boy am I glad to see you. We need to get the accounting system up and running. Your father was asking for some reports the other day and I just can't do it by hand. Call me modern, I guess." He paused, smiling sheepishly, and looked at me and Rudy, as if truly noticing us for the first time.

Kenji spoke up. "These are my two friends from Lahaina, Rudy and K.C. Guys, this is my cousin, Hideyoshi Nakahashi."

"Pleased to meet you K.C., Rudy."

"Likewise."

We shook hands all around and then Hide turned his attention back to the boxes. He glanced uncertainly at Kenji. "Could you maybe give me a hand setting this stuff up? I'm not as good with the technical side of computers as you are. But I'm a devil with a spreadsheet, of course."

"No problem, cuz," Kenji replied good-naturedly. Hide's face relaxed into a full smile and Kenji and Rudy brought the computer to the office area of the restaurant, a small sunny room with one window facing east. Kenji managed to assemble the computer in record time. After only a moment of watching him at work it was obvious to me that he was very knowledgable about the hardware. I thought to myself, "Sushi chef, techie, tour guide, hey, this guy is one class act! Good-looking, too."

In short order, Kenji finished plugging all the wires into the odd-looking sockets at the back of the computer, brushed his hands off and stood up. "That should do it, we're connected to the power lines and the phone system. Let's beam up to the mother ship." Casually, he flicked the main switch on and the computer whirred into life, accompanied by a soft cheer from Hide.

"Kenji, you saved my life, this should really do it. Tell your father I'll be e-mailing that report to him tomorrow latest, would you?"

Kenji grinned. "Hide, it would be my pleasure."

"Say, are you guys hungry?" Hide suddenly asked, rubbing his own stomach at the same time. At our eager nods, he showed us to a small table in the kitchen and offered around a large plate of little spicy vegetable rolls, called gyoza, as well as some cold noodle and vegetable soup from the refrigerator.

"Help yourself," he invited, and did we ever, washing these surprisingly delicious foods down with bottled soda. I was proud to see that Rudy had gotten the hang of using chopsticks and was wielding them with little or no trouble.

After stuffing our faces in silence for a few minutes, we began to talk. "Hey, Hide, something really weird happened last night," Kenji said, and proceeded to tell his cousin about the events at his father's restaurant the night before.

Hide gasped, his gyoza momentarily forgotten. "Someone threw a molotov cocktail at the restaurant?"

Kenji hastened to reassure him. "Well, luckily they missed the window. The only thing that happened was they set fire to the wooden bench in front of the restaurant.

Lamentable incompetence, I say," he added, in an attempt at humor.

"What does your father have to say about this?" Hide asked, a concerned look on his face.

"Won't say a word," Kenji answered glumly, "but I'm pretty sure it has something to do with the two other fires in town and I think he knows something about those too."

"Well, maybe your father has a good reason for not answering your questions," Hide said slowly, then came to a full stop.

"Oh?" Kenji demanded, then added fiercely, "Hide, if you know something you'd better tell me, and now!"

Hide sighed and spread his hands apologetically. "It's not my place to speak, Kenji. If your father wanted you to know things he would tell you himself."

Kenji addressed Rudy and me suddenly, scowling at his cousin. "Can you believe this? Someone tried to burn our restaurant down last night but nobody in my family will even talk about it!"

Rudy and I exchanged quick glances but said nothing, trying to stay out of what was obviously a family dispute. Hide held up a hand to calm Kenji's outburst. "Listen Kenji, sometimes it's better to let sleeping dogs lie."

"Sleeping dogs!" Kenji exclaimed, his eyes wide with amazement. "You call a molotov cocktail a 'sleeping dog'?" He gazed at Hide in disbelief then ran an agitated hand through his hair.

"Man, I don't believe this." Hide seemed to debate the matter with himself for a moment, then looked at Kenji severely. "All right Kenji. But you have to promise you won't tell anyone else. All right?" Belatedly, he glanced at Rudy and me, and added, "You too."

"Fine." I agreed as Rudy nodded his assent also. Still, Hide seemed reluctant share his information.

"Well?" Kenji prompted impatiently.

Hide held up his hand once more. "All right, all right. There have been rumors lately about some kind of turf war here on Maui." Hide's voice sank to a whisper and instinctively, I glanced over my shoulder. But, of course, there was nothing but the empty room around us. "In fact, some people are saying that the Japanese Yakuza is involved."

7

A CLUE FROM THE PAST

Rudy suddenly piped up, "Yakuza? Wait a minute, isn't that the Japanese mafia?" No doubt he was familiar with the word due to his frequent exposure to (ugh) martial arts movies. Hide rocked his head up and down in confirmation.

Kenji seemed truly surprised. "The Yakuza are here on Maui? But what could that have to do with the fires?"

"It's rumored that both the businesses which were burned down were owned by the Yakuza." Hide lowered his voice even more, adding, "Some people are saying the fires were set to deliberately stop the Yakuza from establishing themselves here on Maui."

"So it really is some kind of turf war," I observed, briefly forgetting my resolve to keep to my own business. "Wild!"

"But what does any of that have to do with our restaurant?" Kenji wondered aloud, "Do you think whoever is trying to torch the Yakuza's businesses made some kind of mistake and targeted our restaurant too?"

"I don't know, Kenji," Hide confessed, "but I do know that ever since I told your father the rumors about the Yakuza he refuses to talk about this subject with me." Hide cleared his throat gruffly and continued, "I got the impression that your father may have some reason to fear the Yakuza."

"*My* father? Are you kidding!?"

Kenji shook his head, firmly denying the possibility of any connection between his father and the Japanese mafia. "No way, he leads a very quiet life."

"He does now. That is so, but I have a feeling it wasn't always so," Hide quietly replied. "Listen Kenji, there are some things your father won't talk about to anyone, including me. When he came to Hawaii twenty years ago, he was a very different person. He's changed a lot since then. He met your mother, settled down with her, and then you were born. You know, life changes people." Hide's eyes grew distant as he remembered the past. "The point I'm trying to make here is that I have never heard your father say anything at all about his life before he came to Maui. It's possible that there's something in his past which none of us know anything about and which he doesn't want to talk about. If that were true, that might be why he chooses not to talk to you about what's happening, not because he doesn't trust you."

Hide finished his story gently, and Kenji was silent for a long moment, "All right, I guess I might buy that. But I still don't see why he won't at least talk about what we can do to stop the arsonist," he eventually said.

The four of us sat there quietly for a while thinking things over, then Rudy squinted across the table at me. "What about you, K.C.?"

"Sure, thanks. They really are delicious," I replied, serenely helping myself to two more gyoza.

Rudy was quick to pounce. "That's not what I meant and you know it, K.C. What's your opinion about all of this business?"

I sighed. Rudy was really putting me on the spot, I mean, I couldn't exactly refuse to help Kenji and Hide, could I? Even if I were officially retired from detecting, it would still be impolite not to participate in the discussion. To be civil, I answered Rudy's question. "Well, if I wanted to find out about who was setting the fires on Maui I'd look up the corporate records for all the businesses which were burned and find out who owned them," I replied.

Rudy eyed me somewhat dubiously and asked, "What good will it do us to find that out? We don't want to know about the victims, we want to find out who perpetrators are."

I explained my reasoning patiently to my logic-challenged brother. "True, but if you figure out who the victims are and if you see any common points between them, you'll be a step closer to identifying who their enemies are. Figure that out you'll probably have a short list of who's been setting the fires."

Kenji smiled at me. "Now there's an interesting approach," he said. "You know, I think K.C.'s right. I'd sure like to find out the registration information on the businesses which were burned down. Let's see now, one of the fires last week was at a place called the Starfire Danceteria and the other one was at mahjong parlor called the Lucky Piece. They're both in Lahaina."

Hide was obviously puzzled, and asked, "How does that help us?"

"Well, like K.C. said, since we know the names of the businesses which were burned down we can call the Secretary of State's office and find out who owns them. Once we know that we can go and talk to the owners to maybe see if they have enemies, competitors, maybe that way find out who the arsonist might be. It's a gamble, sure, but it just might work." As he spoke, Kenji was already flipping through the blue pages of the phone book, where the government departments were listed. "This should be interesting," he said.

Kenji dialed the Secretary of State's number, then mouthed his responses to the automated answering attendant's irritating questions and choices ("press '1' if you want to leave a message for the governor's pet parrot! and so forth.). We all waited in suspense. "Ah, a real person," Kenji suddenly said in a different tone of voice. "Hello, I'm interested in finding out the names of the owners for two businesses on Maui. They're called the Starfire Danceteria and The Lucky Piece. Yes, I can hold."

A moment later he nodded at the phone, saying, "Sure, go ahead." Kenji scribbled something on the phone book then paused, a frown shadowing his face. "Could you repeat that?" he asked politely. "I see. Are you sure?" He frowned now. "I see. Thank you." Kenji hung up the phone and stared down at his notes.

"What's up?" Rudy encouraged him to share the information.

"Both businesses were owned by KoSa Kaisha, Inc.," Kenji told us, "and get this," (here he pushed the phone book forward for us all to see what he'd written there), "some guy named Tadao Saito is the sole owner of KoSa Kaisha, Inc. But guess who's the registered agent for KoSa Kaisha here on Maui?"

"Who?" I asked breathlessly, no longer pretending not to be interested in the matter. I couldn't help myself and besides, it wasn't like I was actually getting involved in anything really dangerous. We were all just sitting around talking.

"Hiroshi Saito."

"Hiroshi Saito, huh?" That was a shocker. "Isn't that the same guy who was at your restaurant last night? Didn't your father call him by that name?"

"You got it," Kenji replied grimly.

We stared at each other uneasily as the implications began to sink in. If what Hide had told us was true and the businesses which had been burned down were connected to the Yakuza, then that meant Hiroshi was the one with the Yakuza connections.

"Could it be some sort of an insurance scam? Could Hiroshi be the arsonist?" I theorized out loud.

Kenji's eyes narrowed thoughtfully. "You mean, could Hiroshi be burning down his own businesses for the fire insurance payoff?"

I nodded, but Kenji shook his head. "Not likely. All of the fires have been clear-cut cases of arson. The fires were all caused by molotov cocktails and in cases of obvious arson like that the insurance companies usually don't pay off. Or if they do it's only after months of investigating, so it wouldn't be a very good get-rich-quick scheme."

"Which Hiroshi knows, so he also knows he would have nothing to gain by burning down his own businesses for an insurance payoff," I spoke the logical conclusion lamely, belatedly remembering that I had intended to stay out of the details of the discussion. (Oh well, just talking about what was going on couldn't hurt, right? It wasn't like I was actually getting *involved*.)

"Which brings us back to figuring out who the arsonist is," Rudy said after a moment. "Let's look at it this way.

We know Hiroshi's a jerk, right? Maybe he made someone here on Maui really angry, someone who wants to put him out of business now."

"Which could be any one of a number of people." I murmured. "Given the way he acts, Hiroshi probably has plenty of enemies."

"But none of this explains why anyone would want to burn down your father's restaurant," Hide repeated to Kenji.

"Well, the attack on our restaurant could have been a mistake," Kenji suggested, "maybe the arsonist saw Hiroshi having dinner at our Sushi Ya last night and assumed he owned it. So they tried to burn it down, the same way they burned down Hiroshi's other businesses. Maybe when we figure out who the arsonist is we can tell them they made a mistake. We can tell them that the Sushi Ya doesn't have anything to do with the mafia."

There was a short pause and then Rudy added uncomfortably, "at least we *think* that your restaurant doesn't have anything to do with the Yakuza." He finished his sentence just a little too quickly and I knew he was remembering what Hide had told us about Kenji's father's mysterious past.

The heavy silence at the table was threatening to become really oppressive. "I wish my dad would just talk to me," Kenji muttered, "If there's something in his background he doesn't want to tell me about then fine, he doesn't have to. But this is the present and we have to deal with what's happening to us in the here and now."

"I wonder where your father knows Hiroshi from?" I asked quietly, remembering the brief confrontation between the two men at the Murayama's restaurant the night before. "It sure seemed like they knew each other from somewhere."

Kenji met my eyes thoughtfully. "You know, K.C., you're right. I guess I just assumed that he recognized Hiroshi because Hiroshi had been to the restaurant before. But maybe he does know Hiroshi from somewhere else."

We discussed the matter at length but came no nearer to answering the question of why someone would want to burn down the Murayama Sushi Ya. Eventually, Kenji glanced at his watch then up at Rudy and me.

"Hey guys, we'd better get going if we don't want to be late getting back." Kenji then turned to Hide, saying "Thanks for lunch, and let me know how the computer is working out for you, OK? Call if you have any trouble with those reports."

Hide clapped him on the shoulder. "That I will, cousin. And thanks for hauling it all the way out here for me."

"No problem," Kenji said over his shoulder. Rudy, Kenji and I got back into the vehicle and after another quick glance at his watch, Kenji shook his head regretfully. "I'm sorry, but it looks like we won't really have time to check out O'heo Gulch or anything like that this afternoon. I have to get back in time to open the restaurant in Lahaina."

"No sweat, Kenji," Rudy told him, "Trina's exhibition starts at seven, so we have to get back a little early too."

"How come you guys call your mom by her first name?" Kenji asked, as he turned the ignition on. "I could never address my father that way. It's so informal!"

The Flanagan kids looked at each other and smiled. Then Rudy answered for the both of us. "We didn't used to, you know, but since the separation and divorce, so much has happened, mom and Darrell, Dad and Linda, I don't know, it's like, the formality doesn't fit her any more. But our dad, on the other hand, insists we call him 'Father.' I've stopped trying to figure it all out anyway. My feeling is, go with the flow."

On that note, Kenji slipped the car into gear and headed out of Hana, back the way we had come. He and Rudy discussed what we had learned about Hiroshi as we drove. Me, I just looked out at the scenery, trying not to acknowledge that I was getting into something I wasn't sure I wanted to be involved in.

"What the?!" Kenji suddenly exclaimed, pulling the wheel sharply to the right. I glanced away from my side view in time to see a familiar-looking red town car passing on a curve, coming toward us in the right lane. Our lane. If Kenji hadn't swerved in time to avoid the other car we would have collided for sure.

It was such a near miss that I could clearly see the faces of the occupants of the other car. What a shocker! They were the loudmouth, low-life, drinking buddies from Hiroshi's table at the restaurant the night before.

I wasn't the only one with sharp eyes. Kenji had identified them too and he seemed to consider something for a split second before making up his mind. "Those were the same guys with Hiroshi last night! Sorry guys, I need to check this out. There have been too many coincidences around here lately."

Kenji made a careful but fast U-turn (fortunately we were not on the mountain road, where turnarounds are impossible) and headed back toward Hana.

"What exactly are we going to do when we catch up with them?" Rudy asked curiously after a moment had passed and there was no sign of the other car.

"Just check them out." Kenji replied tersely, "There's something funny about the timing here. Think about it, I mean what are a couple of Yakuza thugs doing here in Hana at the same time as us?"

"Maybe they're looking for the arsonists. Or maybe it's really just a coincidence," Rudy suggested.

"Maybe. Maybe. Let's just see," Kenji replied.

"They can't be very far ahead," Rudy observed, buckling his shoulder belt matter-of-factly.

He nodded at the road before us. "What's up ahead?"

"Not much," Kenji replied, "that's why I wonder what they're doing in Hana. There's nothing down this way except a few houses and Auntie Jean's Lunch Wagon. This end of the island is not very developed at all."

"Auntie Jean's what?" I was distracted by the curious name and Kenji's scowl lifted a little as he explained,

"Lunch Wagon. It's a sort of diner where you can stop and get food. Auntie Jean herself is a cool old lady who runs the place. She knows a lot of stories about Maui." His face turned serious again and he shook his head. "But I have a feeling those two aren't planning to pay her a social call."

We passed the turn-off to O'heo Gulch. There was no sign of the town car parked in the crowded lot reserved for tourists so we continued onward, toward that part of the road which was marked strictly off-limits for rental cars in my guidebook. Kenji sounded frustrated. "I don't see them anywhere," he muttered, "they must have turned off onto a side road, or maybe we missed them back at the parking lot."

"I don't think so, Kenji. Just keep going a little farther," Rudy suggested, "They're probably still ahead of us."

After we had driven another mile or so, Kenji said, "The road starts getting, well, crumbly from here on." I sat up straighter in my seat, noticing for the first time that the asphalt under the Wrangler's tires looked old and grey. It was clear that no repair crews had tended to the weather-beaten road in recent years.

"This is cool," Rudy said, appreciating the rough driving conditions. "Check this out, K.C."

Believe me, I was. It was nothing less than spectacular. There was little in the way of vegetation to block our view of the sheer drop to the ocean and the heavy surf pounding the rocky shore hundreds of feet below. Problem was, there wasn't any guardrail, either.

We were rounding the southeastern face of Mt. Haleakala, passing out of lush rain forest into the far end of the island which is largely comprised of volcanic lava fields. Only straggly-looking little shrubs were hardy enough to tough it out on those rocky grey slopes.

A little farther on, the road took yet another turn for the worse, changing from a marginally two-lane width into a definitely one lane-only mountain goat track type of deal. Even worse, it seemed to be barely chiseled into the side of the mountain. There were places where we were no more than four feet from the edge and a nasty straight drop down. Finally Kenji stopped the Jeep and sighed.

"This is as far as I can go without getting into the really rough part of the road. If those guys are up ahead we'll never catch them."

Rudy and I raised our eyebrows at each other. "It gets worse than this?" There was awe in Rudy's voice and Kenji nodded back with Maui pride in his voice.

"There's actually a spot ahead where a part of the road has fallen away into the ocean. You can still drive it but you have to go *really* carefully."

Rudy licked his lips in anticipation and I could sense what was coming next. "Well, we might as well keep going straight since we're already about half way around the island already, right K.C.?" He grinned like a convinced lunatic at me over my shoulder. I sighed.

In addition to his fixations on sports and girls, Rudy has this thing about cars and driving. I knew that some part of him would never be satisfied until he'd actually seen for himself the nasty little stretch of road that Kenji had described for us but I didn't really want to go there myself, to be perfectly honest. I mean like Darrell said, why borrow trouble?

I was opening my mouth to offer my views on the subject when Kenji's eyes widened in alarm. He was looking in the rear view mirror and I saw his eyes watching something approaching from behind. "Uh-oh," he said, shifting the vehcile quickly into gear, "I think we've got trouble."

I glanced back over my shoulder and saw the red town car. It had come out of nowhere, from behind us, and was approaching at a reckless clip!

8

TERROR ON THE MOUNTAIN ROAD

At the last minute, the other car skidded to a stop just behind us. Kenji scowled and beckoned to the driver to back up but he only leered back and revved his engine so much that black exhaust smoke poured out of the back end.

"Just a hunch, Kenji," I remarked nervously, "but I think those guys might be just a little over the top."

"Yes, either crazy or really stupid." As Kenji spoke the driver of the town car revved his engine again, only this time, he eased forward a little, nudging us with his bumper.

"Hey, what does he think he's doing?" Rudy barked, getting a bit riled up. Kenji just shook his head.

"You tell me, man."

The driver of the town car revved his engine yet again, moving forward to bump us a little harder. It seemed as though he was doing his best to intimidate us and (speaking for myself), it was working pretty well.

Rudy turned to glare back from the Jeep at the driver of the other car. "Why don't they just back off? What's their problem?"

"It's probably because of the way my father and I kicked them out of the restaurant last night," Kenji muttered, "maybe they took it personally. One thing's for sure though, this game is over. Buckle up, everyone."

As he finished speaking Kenji revved up our engine and spun out in a cloud of ancient, asphalt dust. The two men in the town car looked startled then pleased by our departure and the driver of the other car hit his accelerator as well, following Kenji's example.

"Uh-oh," I said, to no one in particular. All I had wanted to do was take it easy and have a nice, quiet vacation. Remember? But, somehow, I had still ended up in a car chase on a winding mountain road with no guard rails! Did my life bear some odd kind of curse? As I watched the road ahead of us with fascinated dread I firmly resolved that if I successfully lived through the next few minutes I would never take another vacation again. Ever!

Kenji had obviously driven the road before, and lucky for us, he knew exactly where to slow down and where to blow his horn before rounding corners that were too sharp to see what lay around them, thus warning drivers who might be on the other side of our approach.

The only problem was, we were going way too fast to actually stop in time should anyone, in fact, be in our way on the road ahead. I looked nervously at the steep drop to our left then back over my shoulder at our pursuers and found myself calling upon the demigod, Maui, himself to keep us from skidding over the edge of the road. I generally don't worship Hawaiian gods but its weird what we do when we're in a jam!

Our Jeep had been built for rough terrain but the town car had not and it slowly lost ground behind us, becoming visible only now and again past vicious twists and turns in the road. Suddenly, we were approaching the section of road I recognized from Kenji's earlier description. It was where a huge chunk of asphalt had fallen away into the ocean below, leaving a wide, very dangerous pothole to drive SLOWLY around. Of course, slow wasn't exactly an option for us at this particular point in time.

"Hang on," Kenji warned us. The wheels of the Wrangler's left side seemed to dip and spin for a second as though over empty space but then Kenji hit the accelerator and we pulled around *that* corner without even sounding our horn.

Rudy was visibly shaken but still enjoying himself, "Whoa. Hey, wait a second!" he added, looking back, "Slow down!"

Rudy was watching the road behind us through the rear window, and as he yelled, urgently, Kenji hit the brakes. We all looked back to see the driver of the town car attempt to take the corner Kenji had just navigated. The other driver's mistake was that he didn't pull over far enough to the right to avoid the missing patch of road. I was delighted to see the red town car come to an abrupt stop, its left front wheel solidly trapped in the pothole left by the chunk of missing asphalt.

"Way to go!" Rudy crowed as our pursuer tried to reverse his way out of the pothole. But he couldn't, because the town car was front wheel drive only. I smiled, thinking of how problematic it would be to get the big sedan out of its predicament. I mean, it wasn't like a tow truck would be able to make it down the road or anything. We high-fived all around.

"Nice going, man," Rudy praised Kenji sincerely.

"I didn't do anything, really, those jerks did it to themselves."

Kenji shrugged modestly as he put the Jeep in gear again. "Now let's get out of here. Something tells me our friends back there like to play pretty rough."

"Fine with me," I said quickly.

"Good idea," Rudy put in, simultaneously. None of us wanted to stick around and see what would happen next. For all we knew, the two bullies in the town car could be carrying weapons, and from the way they'd played chicken with us on the road it was clear they meant us no good.

The rest of the road was bumpy but straight and Kenji drove it like an expert, earning both Rudy's and my solid approval for the way he put distance between us and our pursuers. We finished the tortuous trip around the mountain and were crossing the flat lava fields of the southeastern end of Maui, below Haleakala's crest, before anyone spoke again.

"We have to tell the police about this," Rudy remarked eventually but Kenji threw him a cynical look.

"About what? That a car behind us was driving too fast and scared us?"

He shook his head. "I don't think the police would take something like that too seriously, considering how people are always complaining about bad drivers on this road."

Kenji met my eyes in the rear view mirror for a second as Rudy turned around and directed a piercing stare at me. "What do you think we should we do next, K.C.?"

I shrugged and looked away, still hoping somehow to avoid getting in deeper. "This isn't a game, you know," I began slowly, looking out the window. "I mean, people throwing molotov cocktails, chasing us in cars. It seems to me we'd better just drop the whole thing right now and let the police find out about the fires."

"Oh, come on, K.C.!" Rudy scolded me impatiently, "you can do better than that. You're the one with the most experience in crime-fighting here, so why don't you just help us figure this out. *Then* you can retire, all right?" He caught Kenji's puzzled look at this outburst, and explained, "K.C. here is a pretty talented detective. In fact she was the one who caught that Mexican drug smuggler a while ago, Señor Colón. I don't know if you heard about it here in Hawaii but it was big news where we live."

Kenji nodded, his eyes bright with interest as he glanced sideways at me. "I do remember reading about it. But the story only mentioned 'a Canadian teenager'. You were involved in that? Wow."

I nodded, somewhat reluctantly. "Just 'involved,' no way. She solved the whole thing!" Rudy told him, brotherly pride overflowing.

"With a lot of help from my friends and family, including Rudy here," I added quietly.

"K.C.'s pretty talented with stuff like this but she's still feeling a little scared 'cause she almost died in Cancún," Rudy murmured to Kenji, his voice pitched so low that I could tell I wasn't supposed to hear his words. "She's still a little traumatized by the whole thing."

I contradicted him loudly. "Hey, don't worry about me! I'm doing just fine. It's just that I'm beginning to wonder if this is some sort of curse I have to live with. Every time I go on vacation weird stuff just seems to happen. I'm thinking of swearing off vacations forever."

Kenji smiled ruefully at my words. "I take it this isn't exactly how you want to spend your time on Maui?"

I nodded. "Not quite." Then, realizing that this answer might seem a bit ungrateful to the person who had been showing me around his lovely island I added, "Not that I didn't have a great time on our drive to Hana."

Kenji cocked a disbelieving eyebrow at me and replied, "It's all right if you'd prefer not to get involved in all of this, K.C. I can look into it on my own. I'd feel bad if anything happened to either of you two on my account."

"Well, count *me* in, Kenji" Rudy replied indignantly, "*I'm* not afraid of the big, bad Hiroshi and his Formula One thugs."

"Well neither am I," I protested, "I was just trying to stay out of trouble for a change."

"No one's going to force you to do anything you don't want to do, K.C.," Rudy replied stiffly. At that, we let the subject drop and I folded my arms across my chest, thinking things through as we drove back to Lahaina. To say that I felt torn by conflicting feelings would be an understatement.

Naturally, I was interested in finding out why Hiroshi's buddies had hassled us on the road. Maybe it was because they had recognized Kenji as the sushi chef who'd embarrassed them by asking them to leave the restaurant the night before. Maybe it was because they were just plain mean. Maybe something else was going on that we had no idea about. Still, I couldn't help wondering why they would want to harass us. But I also felt a certain wariness about the situation. I mean, I'd learned the hard way that it was best to remain uninvolved with trouble and troublemakers. I had very good personal reasons (and scars) to walk away from it all and not look back once.

On the other hand, I also had good reasons to stick around and help Kenji. He was a nice guy and besides, once Rudy got involved, things could get a little dicey, to say the least. Not that Rudy is an idiot or anything. It's just that when he wants to find something out he often tends to take the most direct route between two points, as though detective work were geometry, which it isn't. He'd need someone more subtle to keep an eye on him, that was for sure.

Then again, there was no way I wanted to get all mixed up with molotov cocktail-throwing strangers and Yakuza thugs with truly sick senses of humor. That's what the police on Maui got paid for, to keep low-lifes like them in line while people like me enjoyed the sun and surf.

By the time we reached Lahaina, all these thoughts spinning out of control in my head had made me dizzy, and I still had failed to resolve my internal conflict. Not only that, but our little detour had cost us the better part of an hour and now we were slightly late getting back to prepare for mom's show opening at Gerard's Gallery.

Kenji slowed to an easy stop in front of our house, and let the engine idle while Rudy and I climbed out. "Well, thanks for everything, guys," Kenji said. See you later?"

"Later," we assured him and then he waved and drove off, in a hurry to get to his job at the Sushi Ya. Rudy and I had barely enough time to shower and change before Trina and Darrell swept in.

Trina bent to give me a kiss while Rudy and I exchanged glances. "How was your day, kids?"

"It was, um, sure interesting," I began somewhat awkwardly as Darrell joined us.

"How was Hana?" he asked and again, Rudy and I exchanged looks. It didn't seem like a good time to tell Trina and Darrell all about our little drive in the country. We were supposed to be getting ready for Trina's opening night and a lengthy explanation would take too much time and after all, this was mom's night. She was the rightful center of attention. I figured Rudy reached the same conclusion, and we just shut up.

"Has anyone seen my glasses?" Trina had been rummaging around in her purse and directed this question to all of us, "You know, the ones with the octagonal rims?" Darrell shook his head and was distracted from the topic of the drive to Hana.

"Where was the last place you remember seeing them, darlin'?" he asked, helpfully. Trina closed her eyes for a moment.

"At the restaurant last night, I might have left them on the table there."

"All right, we'll make a stop at the Murayama Sushi Ya after the opening then. I don't think we'll have time to make it there before the exhibition starts, though. We're running late as it is."

As he spoke, Darrell crossed the room, heading into Trina's bedroom. "Did you check in here, hon'? Sometimes you leave them on the dresser." Trina followed him and Rudy and I were alone.

"I don't know," he said to me finally, "this doesn't really seem like a good time to tell them about what happened today, does it?"

I agreed completely. "No, it doesn't. Maybe later." We nodded at each other somewhat conspiratorially and split up to finish getting ready for the exhibition. As I got dressed, I concentrated on looking forward to the evening ahead, resolutely pushing any and all worries about sinister mafia types aside while getting ready for mom's big night.

I wore a long-sleeved, deep blue cotton gown with

black sandals that Trina and I had picked out for the occasion and Rudy looked pretty darn good in his dark grey suit and black shirt. Darrell had chosen a black suit and tie with a white shirt and Trina herself, the artist after all, wore a sea-green dress made of some kind of gauzy material which floated around her like foam on a wave. She was gorgeous. My mom! And would you believe it, the glasses surfaced just as we were about to leave the house!

9

THE SHOW OPENS

In fact, we all looked so good, it would have been appro
priate for a limo or a taxi to pick us up, but Trina was far
too nervous to wait around, so the four of us walked over to
the gallery. In any case, it wasn't as if a few blocks' walk
down by the waterfront toward the setting sun was a particular hardship.

Gerard's Gallery was brightly lit. I appreciated the way
the stark glass and brass construction of the building shone
through the growing darkness, displaying a roomful of
Trina's works, glowing softly under the special track lighting. Here and there were small groups of well-dressed people, drinks in hand, clustered about the glass sculptures,
murmuring their approval.

"Trina, darling!" Gerard swept across the room toward
us, his wine glass lifted in a toast, "Here she is, everybody!"
There was a rustle of interest throughout the room and
everyone turned to stare at Trina who gulped then smiled,

raising a hand in weak acknowledgement of the polite applause her entrance triggered.

"Thank you all for coming," she said shyly, "I really appreciate this."

Rudy, Darrell, Gerard and I watched proudly as Trina was enfolded in a little crowd of admirers. I even heard someone ask her quite seriously about what had inspired her to design the mobile of delicate steel and sapphire spheres hanging overhead. I couldn't help smiling to myself as Trina replied with a vague wave of her hand,

"Oh, I don't know really, I just started working, and suddenly there it was." When asked what the inspiration for her work is, this is the stock explanation Trina gives. It keeps the conversation going and saves embarrassment, because, as mom always tells me, "Good artists create. They don't spend time wondering where the inspiration came from."

The next two hours were interesting, to say the least. I had never mingled with so many arts-oriented people and I must say that watching them was almost as interesting as studying Trina's work. An older gentleman leaned down and sniffed surreptitiously at a cluster of blown glass flowers in a swirling glass vase. The flowers were quite obviously glass, but that didn't stop his olfactory exploration. He finally smiled to himself in a curious way, made a note on his cocktail napkin and turned away.

A honeymooning couple fell in love with one of Trina's statues, a mischievous looking cherub aiming its golden arrow at a golden star cleverly suspended above it. The newlyweds told Trina that the cherub was the embodiment of their perfect love and I was pleased to see they bought it on the spot.

Two vivacious young women from a Honolulu magazine were present, taking pictures of the sculptures and promising Trina a marvellous full page spread on her work for the cover of their next issue. Trina posed next to several of her larger pieces for an impromptu photo shoot and when that was over she drifted off to speak with an elderly lady who beckoned to her from across the room.

Rudy materialized at my side, whispering urgently, "K.C., we've got trouble! Hiroshi's here." I felt a sinking feeling in the pit of my stomach when I glanced toward the door and saw Hiroshi and his girlfriend, Kimiko, entering the gallery accompanied by the two men who had chased us on the road to Hana. Kimiko was wearing a long, clinging white dress and matching spiked heels. She clutched a small white beaded handbag and to top off her ensemble she wore a perky white hat sporting a huge peacock feather which hovered in the air over her head quite dramatically.

Hiroshi, again, wore a suit tailored to make his shoulders appear wider than his waist. This time it was a tasteless iridescent orange color instead of the previous electric green, and it stood out even more against the backdrop of Trina's work. Hiroshi's two buddies were dressed in more conservative hues and hadn't lost the shades despite the fact that they were indoors. They gazed about themselves somewhat scornfully as they followed Hiroshi and Kimiko into the gallery.

"What's wrong?" Darrell asked Rudy and me sharply, then followed our gaze, his mouth tightening in a grim line when he saw who we were watching. "Oh, right. Mr. Personality."

He glanced at Trina who had, by now, noticed the new arrivals and was studying them with a little apprehension. We watched in silence as Hiroshi reached his paw for a delicate glass sculpture of a lime-green-and-gold dragon on a brass pedestal near the door, hefting it carelessly from one hand to the other like a pineapple while the people around him murmured disapproval.

Hiroshi glanced in Trina's direction with a smug smile and narrowed eyes, then replaced the dragon carelessly on its pedestal. It wobbled there for a moment as though it might fall and Hiroshi made a show of not moving to stabilize it. Fortunately, the little dragon came to rest upright on the pedestal, at which point Gerard came hurrying across the room to interpose himself between Hiroshi and the sculpture.

"No, sir! No, no and no!" Gerard told Hiroshi sternly. "I must ask that you please refrain from touching anything here." He tried to maintain his cool while saying this but it was clear that he was outraged by Hiroshi's deliberately careless handling of the dragon. "Must not touch!" Gerard added forcefully and to my astonishment, he actually waggled a reproving finger at Hiroshi and friends.

"Is that so?" Hiroshi replied much too loudly, and all conversation in the room ceased as people turned to watch the strange tableau. "Why not, sir? Isn't this all," here Hiroshi waved an arm around himself, brushing the little glass dragon carelessly with his sleeve, "for sale?"

"Why, certainly the work is for sale," Gerard replied, flushed, "but these pieces, this art, is very fragile and requires very careful handling."

Darrell had been watching Hiroshi intently, looking more and more disgusted with each passing moment and I could sense the pressure rising. Finally, his lips twisted downward in an uncharacteristic scowl, he glanced at Trina saying, "I'll take care of this."

Without waiting for anyone's approval, Darrell strode

forward to confront Hiroshi. "You interested in anything in particular, friend? Or are you just lookin' for trouble?" His smile was tense and though he spoke very quietly, Hiroshi seemed a little taken aback both by Darrell's direct manner and his six feet of solid muscle. Behind Hiroshi his bodyguards tightened ranks, flanking him and quite obviously ready to rumble.

Hiroshi shrugged and looked around at Trina's work derisively. "I thought I might buy something for my girlfriend, but none of this looks any good. Where are you hiding the good stuff?"

There was a gasp from those standing close enough to hear Hiroshi's words, and I saw people glance at each other and draw together, whispering as they watched the tense little scene play itself out.

Rudy stepped forward to stand just behind Darrell and I saw both of Hiroshi's bodyguards stiffen suddenly as they recognized him from our encounter earlier in the afternoon. Rudy flashed them a victorious smile and folded his arms loosely across his chest as Gerard glanced back and nodded meaningfully to Archie, who joined us from the small crowd of onlookers. For a moment everyone was silent, waiting for the next move. It came from an unexpected corner of the room.

"How about that one over there?" Kimiko spoke suddenly, breaking into the tense silence. With a flip of her hair she tripped daintily across the room toward a side table, her face alight with pleasure at being the center of attention. "I like this one. Very nice," Kimiko burst out and bent to retrieve a bulky glass object from the table. She held it out, presenting it for Hiroshi's approval. "How about this, 'Roshi?" A quickly suppressed titter of surprised laughter swept the room at her words and I saw people turning away to hide their smiles at Kimiko's mistake.

She was holding a glass ashtray, blown in bright red and teal swirls. It was not one of Trina's pieces, but was instead an ordinary ashtray intended for the use of the gallery's guests.

"You know I think this would be perfect for your desk, Hiroshi-chan," Kimiko purred, turning to Gerard. "How much is it?"

I saw his eyes narrow slightly and the corners of his mouth pull tight, as though he were trying not to smile as Kimiko blithely flipped the ashtray over, checking for a price sticker on the bottom.

Someone behind me giggled, breaking the ice and causing a louder ripple of amusement to run through the crowd. Hiroshi's face darkened and he looked around himself suspiciously, trying to figure out why people were laughing. Apparently he didn't catch Kimiko's mistake. The two bodyguards behind him got it though, and shuffled their feet uneasily, adopting a defensive stance and scowling threateningly around at those nearby who were laughing. This only made things worse and I heard someone break into a full throated guffaw which was quickly stifled.

"Put it back!" Hiroshi snarled, finally figuring out that the disturbance was being caused by what Kimiko held in her hands, "We're leaving!"

"But it's beautiful! I want it, Hiroshi," Kimiko protested. That did it. The people in the room exploded into laughter, and I saw one of the girls from the magazine quickly take a picture of Kimiko and the ashtray while grinning from ear to ear.

"I said, we're leaving. Now!"

Hiroshi turned on his heel and with one backward

glower at the room in general he left the Gallery, closely followed by his two bodyguards.

"Please keep the ashtray, as a gift." Gerard told the somewhat confused Kimiko, ushering her gently toward the door.

"Really?" She was pleased. "That's so sweet of you, thanks! Hiroshi-chan look!" She ran after Hiroshi, holding the ashtray carefully in both hands.

"And there goes another satisfied customer." Gerard said after they were gone. Several people chortled at his joke. There was a huge lifting of tension in the room after that. People relaxed and started mingling around again, laughing and talking about what had just happened. I looked for my mother and happily saw a smile break onto her face in obvious relief that her sculptures were safe from Hiroshi's ham-handed advances.

We stayed at the exhibition for about forty-five minutes after that but for me the evening was pretty much ruined. I mean, I'd deliberately tried to forget the events of the day in order to enjoy myself at the exhibition but instead Hiroshi had arrived, bringing with him thoughts of the Yakuza's menacing presence on Maui.

Trina tried to hide it but I think she, too, was worried about what had almost happened. As I watched, Darrell murmured something to her in a low voice, and she gazed up at him with a relieved smile, nodding. A moment later Darrell joined me and Rudy.

"We're headin' home in a few minutes. You two ready?" Rudy and I nodded simultaneously and watched as Trina made a short exit speech which was followed by an enthusiastic wave of applause as we left and then caught a taxi back to the beach house. On the ride home, the subject of Hiroshi came up. "That guy was way too much," Darrell remarked in disgust. "What's his deal anyway?"

"You don't know the half of it," Rudy informed him grimly. "Wait till we tell you what happened today."

"Oh, what happened?" Darrell directed a quizzical look at Rudy as the taxi dropped us off at the house. We were safely inside before Rudy explained what he meant.

"It's a really long story, Darrell, but you know those two goons with Hiroshi?"

Darrell nodded slowly, sending Rudy a sidelong glance as he flicked the house lights on one after another. "His bodyguards. Sure. What about them?"

"Well, they were in Hana today and they, kind of gave us a hard time on the road." Darrell's face tightened as he listened carefully.

"What do you mean, exactly, gave you a hard time?" He was still speaking softly. "You mean as in bad drivin'?"

"They tried to run us off the road," Rudy said flatly, looking to me for confirmation, "didn't they, K.C.?"

"That they did," I confirmed.

"I want to know everything, kids, and right now," Darrell said grimly.

"Well, they pulled up real close to us on the narrow part of the mountain road where it is pretty dangerous, revved their engine, then kind of nudged Kenji's Jeep until he started driving. Kenji lost them on a sharp curve in the road after that and they got stuck in a pothole bigger than their front wheels," Rudy replied.

"Why would they want to do that?" Darrell asked, sounding puzzled.

"We think it's probably because Kenji's dad scared them out of the restaurant last night," Rudy replied. "But that's not all. Remember what Kenji said about the other fires on Maui lately?" Trina gave Darrell a puzzled look and they both nodded as Rudy went on. "Well, we did some checking today and found out that both of the businesses which have been burned down were owned by a corporation called KoSa Kaisha. And guess who just happens to be the registered agent for KoSa Kaisha?"

Rudy cocked an eyebrow at Darrell, waiting expectantly. "Hiroshi Saito?" Darrell ventured.

"Right, and there's more. KoSa Kaisha is rumored to be connected with the Japanese Yakuza."

"Yakuza means mafia," I explained, in case Darrell didn't know the word.

"I know," he nodded, his eyes crinkling in a quick smile. "Well, I'll be... So you think Hiroshi Saito is connected to the Yakuza and the fires are all some sort of great big plot against him?"

Rudy nodded eagerly, his eyes ablaze with excitement as he finished his thought. "It might even be some kind of turf war between the Italian Mafia and the Yakuza, or even the American mafia for that matter!"

Well, that was a bit of stretch, as far as conclusions go! I watched with fascination as Darrell and Trina's face began to assume 'the look of doubt' formerly reserved for *my* theories on strange events. I know that 'look of doubt' very well, having been the recipient of it on many prior occasions. It is the mingled expression of disbelief and worry that other people — usually parents — get when you tell them something they regard as too preposterous for immediate acceptance but which, in my case, almost always proves to be correct. So there!

Having incurred 'the look' so many times in the past, I was well accustomed to the sinking feeling it gives one but Rudy was a newcomer here, and I saw his eyes widen with dismay as he correctly interpreted the expressions on Trina and Darrell's faces. "No really, it's true," Rudy protested weakly then appealed to me, "Tell them, K.C."

"You have to admit it does sound a little far-fetched, Rudy," I pointed out reasonably. He frowned back and pinched his lips. For once, our roles were reversed. Usually it is me going on with an unbelievable story and Rudy sarcastically commenting on how unlikely it all sounds.

"I agree," Darrell told my brother, gently. "Not only that, but it just plain doesn't make sense, Rudy. You just said yourself that you did some checking and that someone has been burning down businesses owned by a Yakuza operation called LoSa, right?"

"KoSa Kaisha, Inc. actually," I put in. Darrell nodded his head.

"All right then, KoSa Kaisha. But Mr. Murayama's restaurant isn't owned by KoSa Kaisha, is it? So why would there be a plot against his Sushi Ya?"

Rudy shrugged, looking at me for support. "Well, we haven't figured the whole thing out yet but it's possible that there might be some sort of connection between Kenji's father and the Yakuza. Remember how Mr. Murayama seemed to recognize Hiroshi in the restaurant? And how Hiroshi reacted?" Rudy was gaining momentum as he spoke and I saw Trina glance at Darrell uneasily as Rudy finished. "Maybe Mr. Murayama has a Yakuza connection of his own and that's why his restaurant was targeted."

Trina sighed. "Rudy, dear," she began patiently, "I can see that you're concerned about what's been happening here the last few days but really, you have to try not to lose perspective on things."

"Huh?" Rudy replied blankly, "I'm not losing perspective at all, mom, in fact I've gained perspective, don't you see? You have to believe me, it's all true!"

I caught his eye as he ended with a wave of his arm, and shook my head at him surreptitiously. I knew from past experience that this kind of discussion would go nowhere, and we would need more tangible evidence to present to Darrell and Trina before they would believe us.

"Even if it is true, that's not what I meant, dear," Trina replied softly. "I mean that you need to take a few steps back from all of this tension and just breathe for a minute. Calm down."

Rudy's brow clouded with frustration at this attempt to soothe him but Trina ignored his frown saying, "I just don't believe you and Kenji and K.C. should be getting mixed up in what's going on. This is turning into something far too dangerous for three children to handle on their own."

"Hey wait a second, *I'm* not getting mixed up in anything," I put in quickly. "I'm retired, remember?" I was a little annoyed by my mother's reference to Rudy and me as "children". Of course, we are her "children", that's for sure, but I hate to think that she still considers us to be immature when we're practically adults already.

Trina smiled at me. "Of course you are, honey. Whether it's you or Kenji or Rudy isn't the point either. The three of you need to stay out of this and let the police find out what's going on, especially since there may be danger at hand."

"But somebody has to help Kenji and his father, mom, don't you see?" Rudy replied, exasperated despite Trina's efforts to mollify him.

Trina switched to logic when mere motherly concern failed to change Rudy's mind. "But how do you know you won't just make things worse? Think about it, Rudy. You said yourself you don't know who the arsonist is. Well if you approach the wrong person the wrong way, who knows? You might make them angry enough to do something really bad to the Murayamas, like burn down their restaurant *and* their house."

"I guess you might have a point there," Rudy had to admit. He looked chagrined and I felt a pang of sympathy for him. After all, no one knew better then I what he was feeling right then.

"I'm with your mother on this one, kids," Darrell put in, "it just isn't a good idea for you to go chasin' around town trying to figure out what a bunch of gangsters are up to."

"My point exactly," I mumbled.

"But—" Rudy began, as 'Darrell shook his head.

"Let me finish, all right? I just think you'll end up in a lick of trouble with that Hiroshi guy. He's obviously a loose cannon, and a loaded one at that. If he shows up at the gallery or the Murayama's restaurant again then it's our concern and we'll take care of it but don't go chasin' around after him, you hear?"

Rudy nodded slowly, his eyes on the floor.

"We do appreciate your concern for Kenji, Rudy," Trina added gently, "but I'd really rather you let the police get to the bottom of this. I just don't think it's safe for you to get mixed up in anything involving people throwing molotov cocktails and burning down buildings."

Rudy listened to these words with an expression of growing frustration on his handsome face.

"Well now who's up for some cocoa?" Trina asked cheerfully, adroitly changing the subject. I hid a smile and watched as Rudy took himself off to his favorite chair, clearly sulking.

"Me, sweetheart," Darrell said.

"Me, too, mom," I put in.

"Yeah, I'd like some," Rudy added quietly. For once he wasn't channel surfing. In fact, the television wasn't even on at all as he sat there deep in thought, looking out across the water. Could thinking be the cure for the boob tube brain-out? After a little while I joined him, not saying a word, taking the chair opposite his. Rudy looked up at my approach, remembered where he was, and an expression of relief crossed his face.

"Oh, good. I wanted to talk to you."

"What's up?"

"What do you think we should do?" Rudy asked me too quietly for Darrell and Trina to hear.

"Rudy, I think Trina and Darrell may have a point about not getting into trouble." He stared at me in disbelief.

"Oh, come on, K.C. Don't tell me you *still* want to be uninvolved after everything that's happened? How can you be so heartless?"

"I guess I—" Here I stopped and spread my hands wordlessly, well aware of the irony of the situation. "Look Rudy, I know how you feel but you have to keep in mind that this is no game."

"I know that!" Rudy snapped. "I mean obviously it's no game!"

"What I mean is someone could get hurt. It just isn't safe."

"You're just getting back at me because of all those times I wouldn't believe you, like in Cancún," Rudy fumed, entirely missing the point.

"I am not!" I objected, "This has nothing to do with that. It's just that, well, I've done this sort of thing before and believe me, it only leads to big trouble. We've both seen that. In fact, it leads to people getting hurt and sometimes even killed. I just think it's a bad idea for us to get any more involved than we already are, you know? I'm not saying we should ditch Kenji, I'm just saying we should do what we can to help the police help the Murayamas."

"Fine! Be that way, Kook Case." Abruptly, Rudy got up and stalked off to his own room, leaving me totally flustered. I hadn't meant to make him mad. I was just being honest with him about my feelings. Sometimes, I guess you just can't win.

In fact, it was starting to look to me like I couldn't win for losing as far as Rudy was concerned. In the past, I had always followed my natural inclinations to get to the bottom of a mystery and Rudy had always scolded me for getting into trouble. And now that I was trying to stay out of trouble, he was scolding me for not getting involved! It was totally unfair and I shook my head in dismay at the twisted logic of my brother's mind.

A little later I emerged from my deep thoughts and saw that Darrell and Trina were looking at me, still worried. "I think I'll turn in now, it's been a long day. See you in the morning."

"Sweet dreams, K.C.." Trina gave me a kiss on the forehead and the two of them watched me head for my room in silence. As soon as I left, I heard them begin talking in low tones about what Rudy and I had told them. I got ready for bed and fell asleep watching the late movie on the television in my room, some thriller in black-and-white from the nineteen forties that had miraculously escaped colorization.

About three hours later I awoke with a start, glancing automatically at the digital display of my alarm clock on the bedside table as I tried to figure out what had awakened me. It was three a.m. and as my brain grasped and tried to make sense of all this I heard the distant wail of approaching fire engines.

I sat up in bed, groggily pushing the hair from my eyes and listening to the ear-piercing scream of the sirens as first one, then a second engine swept by the house. They were traveling down the narrow road towards downtown Lahaina as fast as they could. I slipped into a pair of blue jeans and a sweat-shirt then tiptoed out of my room, colliding solidly with someone else in the darkness of the recreation room.

"Rudy, is that you?" I hissed. The shadowy figure which had nearly knocked me over hissed right back, "K.C.?"

"It's me, Rudy, yes. Did you hear those fire engines?" My eyes had adjusted to the darkness enough so that I could see Rudy nod.

"As if I could miss it. Sounds like there's a fire somewhere close by." As we listened, the wail of the fire engines subsided abruptly.

"I wonder where the fire is?" I added in a whisper. A moment later, both Trina and Darrell joined us. Trina had a white terry cloth robe belted around her waist and looked sleepy but Darrell was wearing black jeans and a denim shirt and had all systems go.

"I just hope it's not the Murayama's Sushi Ya," Rudy commented. "It wouldn't hurt to check it out, just in case." To my surprise, Darrell agreed.

"Might as well. The fire can't be more than a few blocks from here anyway," he remarked, pulling on his shoes, "I'll go with you."

"I think I'll wait here for you all. I'm not awake yet," Trina said, as she stifled a yawn. She watched us through the window as Darrell, Rudy and I left the house, walking quickly in the direction of the fire.

"I think it's this way," Darrell told us and Rudy and I

nodded as we followed him. It wasn't really hard to find the burning building, since even from some distance away I could see where the sky was lit by an odd, orange glow.

I felt a sinking feeling in the pit of my stomach and Rudy licked his lips nervously as we neared Lahainaluna, the street where the Murayama's restaurant was. When we turned off Front Street my worst suspicions were confirmed. The Murayama Sushi Ya was blazing.

10

FIGHTING FIRE WITH FIRE

The two fire engines which had awakened Rudy, Trina, Darrell and me were parked in front of the Sushi Ya, spraying huge quantities of fire-quenching foam onto the roof and side of the building. The fire itself was awesome, a hot, bright spectacle burning the darkness from the night. It crackled with anger and leaped like an acrobat across the front of the restaurant. Although the flames seemed to be contained when we arrived, the firefighters were taking no chances of letting them spread to the neighboring buildings and had blanketed the entire area with flame-retardant foam. Between the fire and the foam, the smell was overwhelming.

The wooden bench in front of the restaurant had been reduced to a charred mess of blackened wood, what with the molotov cocktail the day before and the fire, I thought it safe to say that the poor thing was a total goner. Suddenly, there was a huge crash as a the street-side part of the restaurant's roof caved in. The air was filled with sparks, prompting astounded ooohs and ahhhhs from the watching crowd.

"Hey, Rudy, K.C.." Kenji joined us from out of nowhere, wearing jeans, a shirt and mismatched tennis shoes. He sounded pretty subdued, not at all surprising given the circumstances.

"Are you all right?" Rudy asked. What a question!! Kenji nodded but then shook his head.

"No one was hurt if that's what you mean. But it looks like we're going to have to close up shop for quite a while."

Just then, Mr. Murayama emerged from the darkness, his face expressionless as he watched the flames on the Sushi Ya begin to die down. "We are very lucky that the damage is not greater. Only the front of the restaurant has burned."

"Lucky?" Kenji replied bitterly, "You call this lucky?" Nobody answered him. What could anybody say?

The fire department stayed until the flames were entirely doused and the police had arrived to take our statements. Rudy, Darrell and I told them what we knew, then did the same for the Murayama's insurance adjuster who had hurried to the scene to take pictures and conduct witness interviews. By the time things had settled down it was almost four in the morning.

"It's getting late. Early, I mean." Darrell remarked eventually, glancing at his watch. Trina'll be wondering what happened to us." Dawn was coming to Lahaina now from the windward side of the West Maui mountains, illuminating them from behind with a rich red color which was almost as bright as the fire had been.

"We'd better be going home now," Mr. Murayama said quietly, watching as Kenji tried to hide a huge yawn.

"Hey, listen man, I'm really sorry about your place."

Rudy spoke gruffly as he clapped Kenji on the shoulder.

"Yeah, tell me about it." Kenji replied, choking on the words.

"Call me, Kenji, we'll talk later."

"Later." Kenji left and we all traipsed back to the house in a state of growing exhaustion. Trina was still fast asleep when we let ourselves in, and believe me, none of us wasted any time following her example.

When I woke up around noon the house was silent. I rolled out of bed and showered, then got dressed. Rudy was nowhere to be seen but Darrell and Trina were out on the lanai, sunning themselves in their robes and drinking coffee. I slid the glass doors open and called, "Morning," to them.

Darrell waved at me and Trina called back, "Morning honey. Come on out and join us."

"I will in a minute, mom." I fixed myself a toasted muffin with cream cheese and flipped through The Maui News, looking any mention of the fire. I found what I was looking for in the community news section, buried under a lot of clutter, and I scanned the words quickly.

Late Night Conflagration on Lahainaluna Road

Local residents called the fire department early this morning this morning to report that a fire had broken out in one of downtown Lahaina's popular Japanese restaurants. Investigation is ongoing and police say that arson is suspected.

I put the paper aside and gazed out over the water while I thought about the fire at the Murayama's Sushi Ya. It really angered me that someone had burned their peaceful restaurant while the world slept, a coward who had hidden behind the mask of anonymity and attacked like a sneak in the night.

Kenji and his father were our friends and thanks to some creep, their restaurant and chief source of livelihood had been destroyed. It was a downright lousy thing to do and I was really simmering at the thought that the arsonist might actually get away with what he or she had done.

Naturally the Murayamas would repair the Sushi Ya. A little remodeling, some work on the roof, a thorough cleaning and the place would be good as new. But that wasn't the point. The point was that there was someone out there who had done this thing and who had, so far, gotten away with it. So far, but no further.

I guess it was then that I realized I could no longer refuse to get involved. Whether I liked it or not, it was just my curse to be always in the wrong place at the wrong time. Since I had a talent for detecting and concern for my friends, I had an obligation to do whatever I could to find the arsonist before anyone else got hurt. Maybe you just can't back off in life. Maybe that's it.

The front door slammed loudly behind me, startling me from my noble thoughts. Rudy came bounding into the room, his face flushed with excitement. With no more than a grunt to acknowledge my existence, he raced past me into his bedroom and emerged a few minutes later carrying his binoculars and camera, both of which he stuffed hastily into a shoulder bag.

"What's up?" I studied him, curious.

"Oh, nothing much," he replied vaguely. I looked past him through the front windows to where Kenji was parked in front of the house, waiting.

"Oh? Come on, Rudolph! Spill it."

Rudy glanced at me impatiently. "Never mind, K.C.

Why don't you go lie on the beach and get tanned or something, huh?"

I persisted. "Where are you going with Kenji?" "I can tell you two are up to something, so you might as well tell me."

"Look, Miss Ex-detective, it's no big deal! We're just going to take a look around and see if we can find out anything about this KoSa Kaisha company."

"Well, then I'm going with you," I told him firmly.

"Really? But you said you were retired from detecting," Rudy reminded me. "What made you change your mind?"

I shrugged. "Believe me, I still have reservations about coming out of retirement, but it's not like I can just sit around after someone burned the Murayama's restaurant. Somebody has to stop the insanity, and, well—."

"You mean it?" Rudy eyed me cautiously. "You're really going to pitch in and help?"

I nodded.

"Well, good, I've got my sister back." Rudy grinned at me broadly and reached out to tousle my hair. This was a trick he had picked up from our father, and I ducked but he was too fast. "That's more like the K.C. Flanagan we know and love so well."

"Ugh, stop!" I protested mildly, smiling despite myself as I straightened my hair.

We told Trina and Darrell that we were going for a drive with Kenji (which was no more than the truth) and they waved us off, cautioning us to be back in time for dinner or to call if we wouldn't be.

"Hey, K.C.," Kenji greeted me with raised eyebrows as Rudy and I climbed in, "you coming with us?"

"Yeah."

"I didn't think you wanted to get involved."

"Well, it does go against my better judgment, but someone has to keep an eye on you two," I pointed out. "So, what's the plan?"

"We were just planning to go keep an eye on the KoSa Kaisha office building to see what happens." Rudy began.

"And after that, I want to go in for a closer look if we get a chance," Kenji added. I couldn't find any flaws with this plan, (or rather, lack of a plan) and said nothing as Kenji put the Jeep in gear, heading northwest on Front Street. I had expected the drive to take longer than it did but Hiroshi's office was a mere seven blocks away, just past Kent Street and about half a block away from a large outdoor bronze meditating Buddha sitting facing the beach.

"This is close enough." Kenji parked the in a small lot near the Buddha, hidden from sight behind a building which looked like a small temple. He checked his notebook then pointed at an office building about a block away. "It's that grey building right over there," he explained as Rudy raised his binoculars and I studied the plain structure closely.

It was unremarkable, a four-storey stucco building with square, tinted windows all around. A large, orange banner on one side of the building boasted vacancies and low, affordable monthly payments. I took this advertisement with a huge grain of salt, since 'affordable' rent on Maui means about five arms and three legs anywhere else in the world. The office building did have one nice feature, though. The back of it was built out over the beach and I could see a long pier stretching behind it into the ocean. A sleek, blue-and-white fifty-foot yacht was moored there, bobbing gently on the waves next to a smaller motorboat and two Jetskis.

Rudy lowered his binoculars and glanced first at me

then at Kenji. "Now what?"

"Now we find a place to watch and wait for a while," Kenji said as we climbed out of the Wrangler. "How about that coffee shop over there?" I pointed to a small cafe which was across the street from the KoSa Kaisha office building. Kenji looked a unit commander's efficient half-smile at me and nodded. "Good idea. We'll have a perfect view and an excuse to be there if Hiroshi or his pals come out and see us sitting there."

"Which they hopefully won't," I added quietly.

We crossed the street to the cafe, trying to move quickly past the KoSa Kaisha office so that we wouldn't be observed by anyone inside, but not so quickly that we actually looked sneaky. I noticed that Kenji was carrying a shoulder bag which appeared to contain a laptop computer as well as an assortment of accessories. He offered no explanation for this odd baggage and I didn't ask for one. Never challenge your commanding officer!

"Table for three?" A smiling waitress was offering to give us a table near the front window. In fact, we had our choice of seats since the cafe was nearly deserted. There were only two other people in the cafe, and they were at the lunch counter sitting with their backs toward us. Rudy and Kenji placed orders for French fries and soft drinks while as for myself, I went with a chocolate malt.

The next half-hour passed quietly. We sat in the coffee shop alternating between snacking and talking to pass the time while we watched the featureless building across the street. At first Rudy held a newspaper up in front of himself to hide his face, peeking over the top of it at the front door of the KoSa Kaisha offices. After a while, though, he got tired of this subterfuge and put the paper down with a sigh to simply stare blankly through the window out across the street. "Doesn't look like anything much is going on in there," he remarked after another half-hour had passed. "Is this all we're going to do? I mean, what if there is nothing to see over there?"

Kenji waggled his eyebrows and patted his shoulder bag mysteriously. "Then we move on to phase two," he told us with a grin.

"We do?" Rudy asked.

"What's 'phase two?' " I asked Kenji warily.

" 'Phase two' is where we go inside and try to check out the business files of KoSa Kaisha," Kenji replied breezily.

I felt a twinge of apprehension. "Uh, we do?"

"How is that supposed to help us find out who the arsonist is?" Rudy asked, looking perplexed.

"Well, it might not," Kenji admitted, "but then again it might. It's my guess that the arsonist is some enemy from Hiroshi's past who is out to get him now. If we can get a look at Hiroshi's business files, we can find out who he's been dealing with and that sort of thing. Maybe we can get a list of names or something and go from there."

"Excuse me?" I interrupted politely. "Not to be a party pooper or anything, but would you mind explaining exactly how we're supposed to get a look at their files? Are you suggesting we just walk right up to the front desk and ask if we can see them?"

Kenji fiddled with the salt shaker on the table before him and shook his head, avoiding my eyes. "Well, not exactly that," he began. "What I mean is we have to create some kind of diversion and then when the coast is clear we move in and get what we need."

"You mean breaking and entering?" I asked flatly.

He shook his head hastily then caught my eye and

nodded. "No. Well um, sort of. I guess"

"But that's a serious offense, Kenji." I was speaking from experience. I had done the 'breaking and entering' thing in Cancún, but fortunately, no charges had been brought against me.

Worse, maybe, my father the lawyer, James Flanagan, esq. had given me a sticky lecture about the dangers of disrespecting other people's personal property rights. I was reluctant to risk another such sermon, let alone run the risk of earning myself a juvenile criminal record.

"Yeah, well so is burning down other people's businesses," Kenji replied grimly. "The way I see it, this situation calls for some pretty drastic measures." Kenji's eyes had taken on a determined glint now. "Besides, it's not like we're going to steal or damage anything. We move in, copy what we need and leave. That's all."

Rudy had folded his arms defensively across his chest at my mention of criminal proceedings. "It does seem a little risky," he said, unsure of which way to go with this. "Isn't there another way?"

"Not if we want to find out who's been setting these fires before they burn down our new restaurant in Hana too," Kenji retorted impatiently. Both Rudy and I were silenced. I had forgotten about the implied threat of arson to the Murayama's new Sushi Ya in Hana and I think Rudy had too. "Besides it's only a problem if we get caught," Kenji added after a moment, "which we won't in all the confusion."

"Confusion?" Rudy raised an eyebrow at his friend. "What's your plan?"

Kenji reached into his pocket producing five small smoke bombs, the kind kids use to make big billowing clouds of blue and yellow for fun on national holidays.

"All we have to do is toss one or two of these little babies inside the office and then when people come running out screaming 'Fire!' we go in, check out the files and take off."

Despite my reluctance to commit a chargeable offense, I had to admit that this did seem like a fairly workable plan. "There aren't any open windows, though," I pointed out after a moment's thought. "How exactly do we get the smoke bombs inside the building?"

This one stumped us for a while and as we pondered the problem our waitress approached the table again a little uncertainly to ask if there was anything more we needed. We'd been there long enough to get hungry again so we ordered more food. The waitress looked a bit puzzled when we asked for a pepperoni pizza and more drinks, instead of dessert, but took our orders anyway.

"How about if we go in and ask the receptionist about the vacant office space?" I suggested once the waitress had departed for the kitchen. "We could pretend we're interested in renting or something. Then one of us can ask to use the rest room or something and plant the smoke bombs while the others are talking to her."

Rudy shook his head. "Yeah, but she'll know there's something fishy about that. "I mean, we're sort of young to be asking about office space."

"That's true," I acknowledged.

"Hey, heads up." Kenji pointed across the street and our discussion came to a halt as we quickly turned our eyes in the direction of Hiroshi's building. A red town car appeared from an underground parking garage and pulled up in front of the lobby. Through the front windshield, I could see that the car was driven by the Phillipino-looking man who had been in Hiroshi's party at the Murayama

Sushi Ya the night of the incident with Kenji's dad.

The car itself looked slightly the worse for wear, and there seemed to be an additional dent or two in the body. I smiled to myself at the thought of how much trouble it must have been for Hiroshi's bodyguards to extricate it from the pot-hole on the Hana mountain road. As we watched, Hiroshi himself emerged from inside the office building, closely followed by his two bodyguards, still decked out in their garish sunglasses. They all climbed into the town car which then drove away toward downtown Lahaina.

"Looks like this is our chance. Let's go," Kenji said as he got to his feet at exactly the moment the waitress returned with our pizza and drinks.

"Check please," he told her crisply as she tried to conceal her surprise.

She put the food on the table. "So, will you be taking this with you?" she asked.

"Right, to go please."

The waitress permitted herself a small shrug for the unpredictability of the clientele then obligingly brought our pizza back in a flat white cardboard box, watching us askance as Rudy finished his cola in two big gulps. We split the bill between us and headed across the street toward the lobby of the KoSa Kaisha office building.

Rudy stopped halfway there. "Wait, what about the pizza? And what do we say when we get inside?"

"Say, maybe we can be pizza delivery people," I suggested, suddenly inspired. "We have the pizza, after all. We might as well use it." Kenji nodded.

"You know, that might just work. Okay, I'll go in and pretend to deliver the pizza. Then I'll create a disturbance with the smoke bombs and you two slip in. Got it?"

"Got it," I replied.

"Check," Rudy added, and the three of us fanned out as we approached the office building. The lobby doors were lightly-tinted plate glass, offering a clear view of a pleasant-looking lounge area across from which was a reception desk. A receptionist was seated at the desk and nearby I could see a small, brass plate that said, "Hi, I'm Gillian Munson."

There was something familiar about her, something about her posture that I recognized but couldn't quite place. But when she looked up it came to me in a flash. She was the American woman who had accompanied Hiroshi and his thugs to the Sushi Ya two nights before.

"Kenji, wait!"

I held up a hand to stop Kenji from opening the door to the lobby. "Look at the receptionist. Isn't that the same woman who was with Hiroshi in the restaurant the other night? Won't she recognize you?"

"You're right," Kenji frowned, chewing his lip thoughtfully.

"Maybe I should be the pizza guy instead of Kenji." Rudy suggested. Kenji and I looked at each other then smiled, simultaneously shaking our heads.

"I don't think so."

"Why not?" Rudy protested our unanimous rejection of his idea. "I'd be a great pizza guy!"

"No doubt," I replied, "but that's not the point. And anyway, even if you could pull it off, she got a good look at all three of us at the restaurant, if you recall."

"Why do you say 'even if I could pull it off'? What's that supposed to mean? Don't you think I can do it?" Rudy was still irked that we had voted down his attempt to play the starring role in our drama but Kenji and I ignored him and after a moment he subsided into a silent sulk.

"Hang on a second. I have an idea," Kenji said, and reached into his shoulder bag, rummaging around for a baseball cap and a pair of sunglasses which he put on. With the cap jammed down low over his eyes and the sunglasses blocking half of his face it was hard even for me to recognize him.

"Better?" he asked. Rudy and I nodded. "Then wish me luck."

Kenji opened the lobby doors and strode inside confidently, carrying the pizza box in front of him. Rudy and I hung back, out of the receptionist's line of sight, while we watched Kenji play his part. He walked right up to the reception desk and slapped the pizza box down, mumbling offhandedly to the receptionist. She, in turn, raised her eyebrows politely while listening to him then frowned, shaking her head.

Kenji shrugged, scuffed his foot on the floor irritably then scratched his head and said something else. The receptionist pointed toward a hallway leading discreetly from the lobby. Kenji nodded and left the reception desk, carrying the pizza as he went to use the phone.

"You think this is actually going to work?" Rudy asked after about a minute had passed and there was no sign of Kenji. I shrugged. "Hope so, bro'. We'll see, won't we?" We waited another minute then Rudy nudged me, whispering, "Check it out."

I followed the direction of his eyes and saw a pale cloud of smoke filling the hallway near the public phones. The receptionist hadn't noticed it yet since the smoke hadn't reached the front of the lobby.

A minute later, the smoke thickened enough to drift into the lobby area and the receptionist finally looked up, evidently sensing something amiss. A startled expression crossed her face as she saw what was happening.

She stood up and put her hands over her mouth, her eyes bulging with fright then she shouted something so loudly that Rudy and I could hear it right through the glass.

"Fire! Fire!"

11

MISSION POSSIBLE

Recovering from her moment of panic, the receptionist reached for something under the desk, triggering the fire alarm. Shrill and high-pitched, it added a definite urgency to the situation. Rudy and I opened the lobby door and stepped inside the building, unnoticed.

It was hard to see around us, since the air had filled rapidly with choking clouds of yellow smoke which smelled of sulphur. More and more people appeared in the lobby, wrenched out of their workday routine by the fire alarm and the smoke. In seconds, there was quite a crowd, everyone babbling excitedly as they hurried to leave the building.

When we were sure no one was watching us, Rudy and I headed down the hallway after Kenji.

"Rudy, K.C. Over here!" Kenji's whisper was loud enough to attract our attention, which was a good thing because we might never have found him otherwise.

We hadn't counted on the smoke as a factor which would interfere with our search but it did. I found it hard to see, and furthermore the smoke made my eyes sting terribly. Fortunately for us, the offices of KoSa Kaisha were right on the first floor just past the lobby on the left.

"In here." Kenji led the way inside the KoSa Kaisha company headquarters and closed the door after us. It was quieter inside and the air was fresh. We were alone in a big three-room office.

"Now what?" Rudy was flushed with excitement. We watched as Kenji took off his sunglasses, sitting down at a computer terminal as he opened the bag which held his laptop.

"Now I download their files into my computer while you look for hard copies."

Rudy was mystified. "Hard copies of what?"

"Documents, records, anything like that." Kenji explained. "Make copies if you can on the copier over there, but remember we only have about ten minutes before the fire department gets here. We're looking for anything that tells us about Hiroshi, why he's here on Maui and who might have a grudge against him. Now, go."

Rudy headed for a bank of grey metal filing cabinets on the east side of the room so by default I was left with a smaller group of wooden filing cabinets in a big office near the back.

I got the impression it was Hiroshi's office the moment I walked in. There was a full-length mirror behind the door, a well-stocked liquor cabinet and a small closet to one side filled with the kind of colorful and shiny suits and shirts Hiroshi seemed to prefer.

"Hurry!" Kenji urged us over his shoulder as he connected his laptop to the office computer. "We don't have much time!"

There were three wooden filing cabinets in Hiroshi's office. I opened the first cabinet and thumbed quickly through the files. Billing statements, both payables and receivables. I made copies of a master client list, some purchase orders and a handful of bills then moved on to the next cabinet.

Inside were three metal boxes, unlocked, which contained what looked like stock certificates and something else I didn't have time to study thoroughly. I scooped them up and ran them through the copy machine as well then replaced them carefully inside their metal boxes, trying to make it look as though they were undisturbed.

The third filing cabinet was filled with what looked like correspondence, letters to and from KoSa Kaisha. Figuring that the letters might tell us something useful I grabbed a pile and copied them too.

"Three minutes left and counting," Kenji called from the computer terminal, "How are we doing?"

"Not much here," Rudy called back, "just a bunch of flyers and advertising stuff."

He had apparently discovered the KoSa Kaisha marketing files. The distant sound of approaching sirens reached our ears just then over the shriek of the fire alarm and the three of us looked at each other in consternation.

"One more minute then let's get out of here." Kenji was typing into the keypad of the laptop with frantic speed. "Just one more minute."

"We don't have one more minute!" Rudy had crossed to a window and was peering through the blinds. "We have to leave right now!"

I grabbed the pile of copies I'd made as Kenji nodded and closed the laptop saying, "This will have to do."

Kenji patted his laptop and opened the office door, peering out. The clouds of smoke generated by our smoke bombs were beginning to dissipate and he looked this way and that to make sure we were alone before stepping out into the hallway.

"Over here," he muttered, leading us toward the back of the building where an emergency exit light glowed bright red. I folded and stuffed the stack of copies I carried into my pants pockets as we hurried down a short flight of stairs into the underground parking ramp.

"Come on guys. This way," Kenji said as he sprinted toward the back of the parking area and a stairway leading to the ground level. We exited the side of the building just as the fire department went in through the front door.

"Man! That was close," Rudy breathed as the three of us walked around the building toward the front, where fifty or so unhappy people were standing around in confusion. I saw Gillian standing next to a man dressed in fire-fighting clothes, wringing her hands and talking fast. As I watched, she looked in our direction and stopped talking. Her eyes narrowed suddenly and I had a sinking feeling that she recognized all three of us, especially Kenji since he had removed his sunglasses.

"Don't look now but Gillian's standing right over there," I whispered from the corner of my mouth. "I think she sees us."

"Gillian who?" Rudy hissed, and I whispered back, "The receptionist, her name is Gillian Munson."

"Everybody just act natural." Kenji murmured, turning to mingle with a crowd of bystanders who had gathered nearby to watch the excitement.

"Hey!" someone shouted behind us, "You there! You kids!"

Rudy, Kenji and I glanced at each other in alarm then quickened our pace without looking back. There was quite a crowd and the shout could have been directed toward any number of the people around us (but probably not). It made me uneasy to think we might have been spotted.

We lost ourselves in the crush of people surrounding the building long enough to reach the safety of a small side street and once we were out of sight the three of us took off running as fast as we could down toward the lot where we had parked the Jeep.

"What a rush!" Rudy exclaimed, climbing in as Kenji started the engine. "Now I see why you enjoy this sort of stuff so much, K.C.".

I opened my mouth to reply, but Kenji spoke first. "We have to get stuff this back to my place and look it over. You guys have time? It's only a few blocks from here"

Rudy nodded without looking at me. "Sure, let's do it."

The Murayama's house was about two blocks from their restaurant and we passed the Sushi Ya on our way there. Nobody said a word as we drove by the blackened building, still decked out in bright yellow crime scene tape.

"Make yourselves at home," Kenji told us when we arrived. The house was small, but decorated in such a starkly simple style that it gave me the feeling of being surrounded by all the space in the world. There were two large rooms in the front of the house, one of which was obviously a library, filled with books in both Japanese and English. The other room was furnished with two easy chairs, a sofa and a coffee table arranged cozily before a wide screen TV. Overall, the decor was a comfortable combination of both eastern and western influences.

"Let's see what we've got here," Kenji murmured as he

hooked the laptop into a large computer monitor on a desk in one corner. I spread out the stack of crumpled copies I'd made carefully on the coffee table, studying them as Kenji and Rudy opened the files Kenji had downloaded into his laptop.

The documents which I had assumed were corporate documents were just that, but the surprising thing was that they were for a business entity entirely separate from KoSa Kaisha, Inc. The documents I had copied were for a partnership named Saito & Associates, Inc. "Guys?" I called excitedly. "Come here and take a look at this, would you?"

"In a minute, K.C.," Rudy answered distractedly, hunched over the computer terminal. I shrugged and went back to the task at hand. According to the documents I'd copied, Hiroshi Saito had formed a private partnership owned by six people, each of whom held equal shares in the business. Oddly enough, the names of the partners were Hiroshi Saito, Gillian Munson, Kimiko Mitsunobu, Jimmy Delapinio, Akira Hamai and Saburo Watanabe. Now, I knew that Gillian Munson was the receptionist and quite frankly, I found it puzzling that she would be Hiroshi's equal partner in a new company.

"This is odd," I remarked to no one in particular, "take a look at this."

"Hang on a second, K.C.," Kenji told me over his shoulder. I sighed and flipped through the remaining copies. One set of documents in particular caught my eye. I was very surprised to find that each of the six partners carried life insurance policies in the amount of one million dollars.

"This is really strange," I commented to myself. "Why would they all be insured for this much?"

"What's that, K.C.?" Kenji turned toward me, a question in his eyes. I had his attention at last.

"Take a look at this. Hiroshi formed a new business with five other people." Wordlessly, Kenji and Rudy crossed the room to my side and I showed them the copies I'd made.

Kenji flipped through the copies quickly. "Saito & Associates, Inc.? But why would Hiroshi form a new company when his other business is doing so poorly?"

"Maybe he's doing it to fool whoever's burning down KoSa Kaisha's businesses," Rudy said thoughtfully as Kenji frowned at the names of Hiroshi's partners.

"Gillian Munson?" Kenji shook his head. "This doesn't make any sense at all. Why would she be listed here as Secretary-Treasurer if she's really working as a receptionist? I mean, according to this, even Kimiko is an officer. She's the Accountant. Can she even count?"

"I don't get it either," I told him.

The three of us stared at each other in silence for a moment then Kenji said, "I wonder how Saito & Associates are doing so far in terms of profits?" I glanced at the documents in my hands.

"According to these insurance policies, Saito & Associates, Inc. is turning a profit of $250,000.00 each month." I told Kenji and Rudy.

Kenji turned to the computer with a scowl, rapidly typing in commands. A moment later he said, "That can't be right. According to these computer records there are absolutely no earnings here from Saito & Associates, Inc. How can they have no record of profits if they're making $250,000.00 a month?"

Someone cleared his voice from the doorway, and we all looked up to see Mr. Murayama watching us. He was leaning against the wall just inside the door and it looked as though he'd been there for quite a while. I wondered how much he'd heard. Quickly I shuffled my purloined copies into a neat stack and slid them aside. Mr. Murayama didn't even glance my way but somehow I knew he'd noticed my furtive gesture.

"Oh, hello there, Dad." Kenji stood up quickly, trying for an air of nonchalance. "We were just—"

"I heard. You are prying into things that do not concern you," Mr. Murayama replied tersely. "I told you not to interfere in this, Kenji, didn't I?"

"Dad, you don't understand," Kenji told his father earnestly. "We found out some really interesting things." He glanced at Rudy and me for support and we nodded.

"Oh?" Mr. Murayama was still standing near the door, arms folded across his chest. "And what have you children discovered?"

"That all three of the businesses which burned were owned by a corporation called KoSa Kaisha. KoSa Kaisha is owned by someone called Tadao Saito and Hiroshi Saito is the corporation's registered agent. There's a rumor they're both connected to the Japanese Yakuza, do you know anything about that?" Kenji asked his father. Mr. Murayama stood motionless, looking as though he had suddenly been turned to stone.

"How did you find this out?"

"We called the Secretary of State's office and asked around some. This and that." Kenji tried not to look guilty but failed entirely.

"Why did you disobey me?" Mr. Murayama crossed the room to my side, reaching for the pile of copies I had pushed aside. I didn't even try to stop him when he picked the stack of papers up and flipped through it, his eyes widening as he saw what they were. Kenji stood up and clenched his fists at his sides, facing his father squarely.

"It's time for you to tell me the truth, dad. Is our Sushi Ya somehow connected to the Yakuza? Because if you're in trouble you should tell me, I might be able to help. Or at least find out who's setting these fires before they burn our restaurant in Hana too." Mr. Murayama turned a piercing stare on his son as Kenji continued, quieter now, almost whispering. "Are you in some sort of trouble with the Yakuza, dad?"

"I once led a very different kind of life." Mr. Murayama commented obliquely, "I was not always a sushi chef."

"Oh?" Kenji raised his eyebrows, obviously waiting for an explanation.

"A very long time ago, I worked with Hiroshi Saito," Mr. Murayama admitted, after a pause, "You must trust me when I tell you that it is not a good idea to involve yourself in his business."

"You're hiding something, dad! I can tell!" Kenji exclaimed, getting to his feet in agitation, "What is it?"

12

THE EXILE

* * *

FLASHBACK

Tokyo, Japan. Masataka Murayama and Hiroshi Saito are sitting side by side in deep leather chairs, before a broad mahogany desk. At their backs, a panoramic view of Tokyo city is visible through huge picture windows. Masataka and Hiroshi don't notice the view, though, they are busy ignoring each other. The icy silence between them is massive.

Two heavy mahogany doors swing open across the room and the two young men look up simultaneously as Tadao Saito joins them. He folds his hands before him on the polished wood of his desk and there is absolute silence in the room. For three full minutes, no one says anything. Then finally Hiroshi bursts out, "Well? Aren't you going to say anything?"

Hiroshi points accusingly at Masataka as he continues, "Why haven't you had this one put to death? His carelessness has killed my uncle and yet you still let him live!" Tadao Saito watches this outburst impassively. Another moment passes before he chooses to speak.

"As you know, this has been very difficult." His face expresses nothing of the anguish he feels at his brother's violent death at the hands of the assassin in the mahjong parlor. "Mistakes were made by everyone, myself included." He does nothing to elaborate on this remark but Masataka glances up from the desk to meet his eyes for a moment, surprised to find Tadao's eyes resting on his face in something like sympathy.

"Of course it has been difficult and that's the reason why we should execute this traitor and put the whole thing behind us!" Hiroshi replies indignantly.

He speaks as though he believes his own lie and Masataka's eyes narrow for a second then go blank. He doesn't dare contradict the words of the son of Tokyo's most powerful Yakuza boss for that would mean dishonor to Tadao's son and therefore death for himself. Tadao Saito ignores Hiroshi and watches Masataka in silence.

"You will leave the country and never come back," he addresses Masataka finally. "You are not a member of our organization anymore but there will be no further penalties to you for what has happened. You will be free to make a new life for yourself somewhere else." Masataka gazes up at Tadao Saito, a look of amazement in his eyes at the mercy he is being shown.

"What?" Hiroshi shouts, enraged. "You're letting him go? After what he did?" Hiroshi stands and begins to pace across the room angrily, his fists clenching and unclenching. "He deserves to die!"

"I have heard it said that Hawaii is a nice place to live. "Tadao Saito is still ignoring Hiroshi and speaking only to Masataka. He reaches into his desk for a thick envelope, which he hands to Masataka. "Take this and go. I can do nothing more for you." Masataka stares at the envelope, his eyes widening when he sees that it is full of cash. There is at least one million yen in the envelope, large bills mostly.

It is a generous stipend for one who has been blamed for the death of Tadao Saito's brother and Masataka understands that the money is to buy his silence about what really happened. He knows that by accepting the money and leaving the country he will be accepting the blame for Hiroshi's mistake, thereby saving face for Hiroshi and for his father as well.

The idea of living the rest of his life as Hiroshi's scapegoat is not appealing but as the alternative could well be death, Masataka bows humbly and accepts the envelope from Tadao Saito's hand.

Hiroshi is practically livid with rage. "You're giving him money now, too? You old fool." He shakes his head, speaking without thinking as usual, "When I am in charge things will be different, I will—" Hiroshi stops in mid sentence, suddenly realizing that he has said far too much.

"But you are not in charge." Tadao stands slowly and faces his son unflinchingly. "Perhaps you never will be." Hiroshi's face drains of color and he gapes at his father uncomprehendingly. "You make too many mistakes, *omae*. You disappoint me. You failed to protect my brother and then lied to me, blaming Masataka for your mistake." Hiroshi's jaw drops open and he gulps for air like a stranded fish. Masataka's face is expressionless at he listens to this exchange.

"What do you mean I lied?" Hiroshi stutters, "I told you what happened, I told you.."

"You told me lies," Tadao Saito snaps, weary of his son's stupidity. "We both know who was supposed to be guarding the front door of the hotel."

"It was Masataka—" Hiroshi begins weakly, but Tadao cuts him off with a curt gesture.

"Who takes the blame for your mistake. And this is why I will send him to Hawaii instead of having him punished."

"But, but—" Hiroshi stammers then falls silent, humiliated by having to face the truth. Tadao looks over at Masataka, his face stern and gentle at the same time.

"Go now." He says finally and Masataka heads for the door, casting Hiroshi one last look of loathing. Before he leaves, Masataka turns and bows gratefully to Tadao, very low and deep. To his absolute amazement, Tadao returns the gesture. Masataka Murayama squares his shoulders and leaves the room without looking back. Tadao Saito watches him go, then turns to Hiroshi.

"And as for you, *omae,* this is the last time you will be trusted with anything important. You make too far many mistakes for that.

"What do you mean?" Hiroshi is stunned. Tadao shakes his head and passes a hand wearily across his eyes, swiveling his chair so that he faces the huge picture windows.

"Get out." Tadao says suddenly, uncharacteristically forthright with his bumbling son. "We will talk about this later. Leave me now." Tadao stares out over the twinkling lights of the city of Tokyo as Hiroshi gets hastily to his feet, backing toward the door and nearly falling when he tries to bow humbly to his father at the same time. His departure is not nearly so graceful as Masataka's was and Tadao Saito never even looks in his direction as Hiroshi leaves the room.

***

"I cannot tell you everything. For now I ask you to trust me," Mr. Murayama told Kenji firmly. "I will handle this situation myself."

"Oh, yeah?" Kenji shook his head and slammed the lid of his laptop down much harder than necessary. "Fine. Then why don't you tell me about your plan to save the restaurant in Hana? Because if someone doesn't do something soon I have the feeling there won't be any restaurant left to save!" Kenji stalked angrily out of the room. After an embarrassed look at each other Rudy and I said goodbye to Mr. Murayama and followed Kenji outside.

"You all right?" Rudy asked Kenji quietly when we caught up with him at the Jeep. Kenji didn't look all right to me, in fact he looked furious but he nodded anyway.

"Yeah, sure, I'm fine. It's just that I hate when he does that. I wish he'd just level with me, whatever the problem is." Kenji massaged his right shoulder wearily with one hand, "Hey, thanks, you guys. I think we did a pretty good job today." He and Rudy slapped hands in self-congratulation while I shook my head.

"I hate to tell you this, but I'm afraid we have a little problem. I'm pretty sure Gillian recognized us when we were leaving, remember?"

"Oh, yeah," Rudy's triumphant smile faded, "That's right. She did." He looked somewhat crestfallen as I continued, "I bet she'll put two and two together and realize we were involved once they figure out that the 'fire' was caused by a smoke bomb."

Kenji looked worried as he climbed into the vehicle. "If they do figure that out Hiroshi's going to be pretty mad. But chances are they won't, right?" He put the car in gear. "Look, I have to get going here, I'd give you a ride home but I have a couple of errands to run."

"Call me later," Rudy replied, "maybe we can hook up." Kenji nodded and flashed us a smile as he pulled away from the curb.

Rudy and I walked slowly along the waterfront toward the house. "Pretty interesting day," Rudy observed.

"That's for sure," I agreed. We walked another block in silence.

"They can't prove we were the ones who broke in," Rudy remarked eventually, "right?"

"That's not the point," I reminded him patiently. "If they figure out it was us who planted the smoke bombs we'll be in trouble. Maybe they'll break into Gerard's Gallery and trash all of Trina's sculptures or something." Rudy was silent for a long time.

"You really think they'd do something like that?"

"Hiroshi? I wouldn't put it past him. I mean, he's already probably pretty paranoid about the fact that someone has been burning down his businesses. Maybe he'll flip out and think we're the ones who have been setting the fires."

"Oh, great! So that means now we have Hiroshi after

us *and* the arsonists after Kenji and his father," Rudy concluded. "Maybe it wasn't such a good idea to break into the office after all."

I sighed, "Look Rudy, I think we should tell Trina and Darrell what happened today. Come clean, you know? Or at least warn them somehow about the gallery." I didn't have time to elaborate on this point since, by that time, we had arrived at the house.

Trina called cheerfully from inside the recreation room, "Is that you, kids? Come on in. How was your day?" Rudy and I traded glances then went inside.

"It was, um, interesting, I guess," Rudy replied. Darrell was sitting with his feet propped up on a wicker ottoman, reading the paper. He glanced up at the two of us over the narrow reading glasses perched on his nose, evidently alerted by something in Rudy's tone of voice.

"Oh?" he prompted, "do tell." He put the newspaper aside as Trina drifted back to her work in progress. She had spread a canvas tarp over the floor and upon it stood an easel. I was delighted to see that she had been dabbling in watercolors. Trina is unsurpassed in watercolors but she rarely paints with them. She once told me that working with watercolors makes her feel too impermanent.

"Well, we sort of went driving with Kenji and we, um, we—" here Rudy licked his lips and shrugged, "well, you see it's like this." His procrastination had earned him the undivided attention of both Trina and Darrell. "We sort of um—" Rudy came to a full stop, looking at me with something akin to desperation in his eyes.

"We created a diversion with smoke bombs, entered the KoSa Kaisha offices without their permission and copied their files," I told them both bluntly. "Oh, and we also had lunch with Kenji. Place across the street from Kosa makes great malts."

I braced myself for the storm, but instead of an angry parental outburst, Darrell just stared at me unemotionally for a second or two, then slowly reached up to remove his reading glasses. "Run that by me again, K.C.," he said finally. "Not the part about lunch. The part about breaking into the office building."

Trina carefully swirled her brush free of paint and removed her smock, hanging it over one end of the easel. "Did I understand you to say you broke in to the building and copied their files illegally?"

This question was to Rudy who he nodded apologetically, looking more or less at his shoes as he muttered, "Well, yes."

"All right," Trina said reasonably, "let's have it. The whole story. I'd like to hear it from you, Rudy, if you don't mind."

Her absolute calm actually made whole the thing worse. Under her measuring gaze, Rudy told Trina the entire story, if rather haltingly, finishing up with, "So it wasn't like we stole or broke anything. All we were doing was finding out about KoSa Kaisha so we can stop whoever is setting the fires before they can burn down the Murayama's Sushi Ya in Hana." "Anyway we, well... there's a chance we were recognized by the receptionist. She was at the restaurant a couple night ago when we were there and she might have seen us leaving the building. We're telling you all this because, well...it's like this, you see we—" He paused again awkwardly and I finished the sentence for him.

"We don't want anything to happen to Trina's sculptures. If Hiroshi finds out it was us who broke into his office today, he might try to retaliate or something."

There was silence in the room as Darrell and Trina

exchanged a long look. Trina chose her next words very carefully. "Now listen kids, I'm assuming you don't expect us to tell you what you did was all right, because it wasn't. You already know it was wrong, and even worse, it was just plain stupid. Are we on the same channel here?"

"Right, mom."

"Right."

Rudy and I nodded, looking downwards, neither of us interested in seeing the disappointed expression on Trina's face.

"I know you're worried about your friend Kenji and I think it's terrible what happened to the Murayama's restaurant last night but breaking into someone else's office is not the solution to this problem." Trina's voice had taken on the same tone she used to rebuke us years ago when Rudy and I were little kids and went out exploring without permission. It was a tone of voice which automatically made us hang our heads.

Rudy blurted out suddenly, "Look, I'm really sorry we did something so dangerous but if we don't figure out who the arsonist is they'll burn down the Murayama's other restaurant too and then Kenji and Mr. Murayama will be in even worse trouble. Besides, it's not as though Hiroshi is such a nice guy anyway. I mean look what a jerk he was at the gallery and when his hired hands chased us on the road."

Trina sighed, "But we live in a civilized society, Rudy, and the thing that makes it civilized is that we've all agreed to abide by certain rules. When you start breaking the rules, you lose the right to be protected by them. I guess I can understand how you feel," she added finally, "but I still think it's time for you to start acting more like adults, especially you, Rudy. I mean it's one thing when it's K.C.

who's running around getting into trouble. She's still just a little kid. But when you start doing it too, well I.... I can't help being a little disappointed."

I sat bolt upright in my chair. "Hey, wait a minute here! I resent that! I'm not just a little kid anymore, you know." As no one replied, I threw in, "And besides, I do not 'run around getting into trouble' either. I should think you'd know that by now. Gee whiz! We were just trying to help Kenji and his father."

"I see you've come out of retirement, K.C.," Darrell broke into the crashing silence that followed mom's words. "What do you suggest we do next?" He was probably humoring me, but I answered him seriously anyway.

"I think we need to hire a guard to watch the gallery at night."

"That's already been taken care of, K.C.," Darrell replied in a matter-of-fact way.

"Really?" I was quite surprised. "How's that?"

"I hired a guard for the gallery last night right after the exhibition. Couldn't bear to think about my sweet darlin's work bein' trashed by a bunch of nasty Japanese ruffians."

Trina was genuinely surprised, and touched. "You did that for me?

"Sure did, darlin'. Too bad I didn't think of havin' someone keep an eye on the Murayama's Sushi restaurant, too."

"That's just so sweet." Trina smiled at him with tears in her eyes, but her smile faded again as she looked back at me and Rudy.

"I want you to promise me you'll never anything like this again, do you understand me?" Rudy nodded remorsefully as our mother continued in a very stern voice, "And I want you to mail those files or whatever it was you took back to the office you broke into. They'll be needing them."

"Actually, we made copies, mom," I informed her coolly, still stung by her earlier reference to my immaturity. "Nobody took anything. Kenji downloaded stuff into his laptop and I made copies of the corporate documents."

There was a brief silence then Darrell offered, "I think the best thing for us to do is just sit tight, see what happens. I'm actually glad you two decided to come clean about this whole thing and warn us. At least you did that part right."

"Uh, thanks, Darrell, I appreciate your support," Rudy responded, uncertain of what was coming down the pike after the compliment.

Darrell hardly missed a beat, adding, "Because now that we know there might be trouble we can take steps to really protect ourselves. I'll hire another guard. In fact I'll hire two while I'm at it. See if we can keep the lid on this mess." As he spoke Darrell unfolded himself lazily from his chair and reached for the telephone. "Excuse me for a moment, please," he told us politely as he dialed.

Rudy, Trina and I watched in bemusement as Darrell had a brief conversation with someone on the other end of the line. "Yeah, it's me. Say, I need another favor." Darrell half turned away but we could still more or less hear him. "I'm goin' to need more help with that problem I told you about. Yeah, that's right. Say, two more men." He listened for a minute. "That'll be fine. Good. And thanks buddy, I owe you one." Darrell put the phone down and turned to find us all watching him in total silence. "That's that, then."

He smiled blandly as though unaware of our fascinated stares and settled himself into his chair again, tousling Trina's hair gently on the way down. "It's all been taken care of. A couple of friends of mine will be keepin' an eye

on the Murayama's restaurant in Hana and watchin' the
gallery for us, darlin'. So you all can relax now."

"You said two *more* men," I remembered. "If you have
one guy watching the gallery and one guy watching the
restaurant in Hana what's the third guy going to be doing?" Darrell's eyes were unreadable as he turned to me.

"Why, K.C. honey, he'll be keepin' an eye on the house
here, just in case."

"Oh," I gulped, suddenly realizing what this implied.
Rudy got it too and we sat there together looking hard at
Darrell.

"Relax, kids. It's just a small precaution. Nothing to
worry about. Now who's up for a picnic on the beach?" He
changed the subject adroitly, lightly bullying Trina, Rudy
and me into concentrating on the topic of our evening
meal until we were past that awkward moment where we'd
all realized we might be in serious danger.

13

SUKI'S PLACE

The rest of the afternoon passed quietly enough after that. We all sat around making polite small talk and pretending we weren't at all worried about Hiroshi, the mysterious arsonist, or anything like that. It was tricky but we all managed to avoid any mention of topics relating to the trouble we were in until the sun started setting. The reason I mention the sunset is because that was when Trina got that faraway look in her eyes as she gazed up at the sky. When she turned away from the window I recognized the expression on her face, a combination of excitement and determination.

"Darrell, could you give me a hand with my easel? Those colors aren't going to last forever and I want a chance to paint them before the sun sets any further."

"No problem, sugar'."

Darrell slung Trina's easel over his shoulder while she gathered up her watercolors. After cautioning Rudy and me to take it easy, the two of them went out on the beach for a sunset painting session. Not long after they left the room, the phone rang. Rudy practically hurdled the television in his haste to answer it.

"Hello?" Oh hi, Kenji. I was just thinking about calling you. You did? Well?" Rudy nodded into the receiver. "What? He did? That's weird. You're right. It probably is. Uh, huh. Okay, we'll be right over." Rudy hung up the phone with an odd look on his face.

"So what gives?" I asked.

"That was Kenji."

"Duh," I told him equably. "So what did Kenji have to say?"

"Kenji had a big fight with his father this afternoon. He says his father acted really weird. Wouldn't answer any of Kenji's questions but told Kenji he should just stay home until he called him then left. Anyway the point, is Kenji was looking through the files he downloaded in Hiroshi's office and he found something he wants us to see."

"Like what?"

"Well, he didn't say exactly. But he said it would take too long to explain and he wants to keep the phone line open in case his father calls him."

"So, we're going over there now."

A quick glance up and down the beach showed me that Trina and Darrell were nowhere in sight. So I scribbled a quick note for them to explain where Rudy and I were going.

It did occur to me that Trina and Darrell might not exactly approve of our visit to Kenji's place. That was true. But it was only a visit to a friend's house, after all. I mean it wasn't like we were going to get into any trouble on a harmless errand like that, right? Rudy and I hurried so it took us only a few minutes to reach the Murayama's house. Kenji answered the doorbell on the first ring and showed us inside.

"Any word from your father?" Rudy asked.

Kenji shook his head. "Not yet. I'm starting to wonder if something has happened to him." He cast a quick glance up and down the empty street behind us and then closed the door. "Check this out."

Kenji had his computer up and running on a desk across the room and all around it were spread the copies I'd made during our break-in at KoSa Kaisha. "I found out that besides The Lucky Piece and the Starfire Danceteria, KoSa Kaisha owns one more business on Maui, a night-club called Suki's Place right here in Lahaina." I crossed the room to look over Kenji's shoulder at the display of billing statements on the computer monitor.

"So there's one KoSa Kaisha company left that hasn't been burned down yet?" Rudy asked.

Kenji reached for a stack of computer printouts, nodding. "So far. But if my guess is right, Suki's Place will be the next. Maybe even tonight." Kenji's eyes narrowed and I saw him lock gazes with Rudy. "Maybe if we keep an eye on Suki's Place long enough we'll catch whoever's been setting all these fires when they try to burn it down."

"So all we have to do is wait until the arsonist shows up and we'll be able to figure out he or she is, right?"

"Right," Kenji nodded, "and then we call the police."

"End of story." Rudy grinned, pleased with their solution.

"I'm not so sure that's such a good idea, guys," I said. Rudy gave me a surprised look.

"You don't think it's a good idea just to go take a look at Suki's Place?" Kenji asked.

I arched a brow at him quizzically, and replied, "You mean just like the way we 'took a look at' the KoSa Kaisha office building this afternoon?" Kenji's eyes dropped and he shrugged sheepishly.

"This time we'll find a hiding place outside the build-ing and just watch. I promise, K.C. Really, we'll just watch," he repeated.

"Sure we will," I nodded in polite but total disbelief.

"No, really, we'll be perfectly safe," Kenji insisted.

"If you say so," I said, "but just in case, I'm calling and leaving a message for Trina and Darrell to let them know where we'll be."

"You're can't tell them that, K.C. Trina will have a hissy-fit! Remember, they told us to stay out of trouble!" I firmly faced Rudy's objections.

"Listen bro, you have to trust me on this one, all right? You wanted my professional advice and so here it is. I say it's a good idea for us to let someone else know where we'll be in case things go wrong. And anyway, all we'll tell Trina and Darrell is that we're going someplace called Suki's Place. We don't have to tell them what *for*, exactly."

Rudy nodded reluctantly. "I guess you have a point there." He and Kenji waited while I left this message on the machine at the beach house, carefully avoiding the subject of why we were going to Suki's Place. I knew full well that Darrell and Trina would be really angry if they knew that we were planning to hang around one of Hiroshi's nightclubs after they had expressly instructed us to stay away from him. But under the circumstances it wasn't like we had any real options, exactly.

The arsonist had to be stopped, which meant we had to watch Suki's Place and see who showed up to burn it down. I knew that if Rudy and I had a chance to sit down and explain things to my mother and Darrell they would understand the urgency of the situation and agree that what we were about to do was the best course of action. (Or at least, this is what I told myself to relieve the guilty feeling which still lurked in the pit of my stomach as I hung up the phone). Lying by leaving something important out seems to be as bad as lying by changing part of the story that stays in, I guess. I wonder what I would do if I was a president, or prime minister...

Suki's Place was in a part of town called Lahaina Center, about two blocks from the Murayama's house so Rudy, Kenji and I walked there, taking a short-cut over on Wainee Street. The nightclub itself was on the corner of a block of several restaurants, bars and clubs all side by side in a row along the street.

"That's it." Kenji whispered, pointing, and we all walked slowly closer to the entrance. Since the front of Suki's Place consisted of mirrored glass picture windows, it was difficult to tell anything about the place at all from the outside except that it was not yet open for business.

"Let's check out the alleyway," Kenji whispered even though there was no one around to hear us.

"Good idea," Rudy agreed, "maybe there's somewhere back there where we can hide while we watch the place." Rudy and Kenji hurried around the side of the building, heading for the narrow alleyway behind Suki's Place while I uneasily watched them go. To tell the truth, I had a bad feeling in the pit of my stomach.

"Hey, guys!" I called. "Wouldn't we be better off watching the place from over there, across the street or something?" Kenji and Rudy paused, considering my words, then Kenji shook his head.

"We won't be able to see much from that far away, K.C. This will be much better." Despite my reservations, it was perfectly clear that Kenji had a valid point. I followed the two of them reluctantly, still uneasy about what we were doing.

"Don't worry, K.C.," Rudy told me over his shoulder as we turned the corner into the dark, narrow alleyway, "There's nothing to be frightened of. We'll be perfectly safe."

It was truly a moment to remember, for just as Rudy spoke these words we came face-to-face with Hiroshi's body-guards. They were coming out of the back door to Suki's Place just as we reached the alleyway and they stopped dead in their tracks, looking blankly through their sun-glasses at the three of us. For a moment everyone was fro-zen in place.

I looked around desperately for a place to run as the tallest bodyguard slipped his hand into his pocket and over a bulky object that gave me the chills. Through the material of his jacket, the object took on the very ugly shape of a gun. Pointing at us.

"Oh, crap," Rudy muttered. The two men glanced at each other silently then and I saw a slow smile start on the tallest one's face. "This must be our lucky day, we were just on our way to look for you brats. Mr. Saito wants to have a little talk with you."

Kenji backed up slowly. In fact, all three of us were edging cautiously toward the street, trying to pretend that there wasn't a gun pointed at us. "Does he really? And what if we don't want to have a little talk with Mr. Saito?"

"This little friend of mine here says you will anyway, so stick around, and don't even think of trying to run off anywhere." The tall one tapped the gun in his pocket loudly, and we all stopped in our tracks.

"You're in luck, not far to go. Mr. Saito is right upstairs." The shorter bodyguard opened the door leading to the in-side of Suki's Place and waved us inside. Kenji, Rudy and I glanced at each other, making no move to comply. The tall bodyguard waggled his gun threateningly in his pocket.

"So sorry. You gonna go in by yourself or do I have to use this?"

Kenji shot him a resentful look but obeyed, walking into the darkness of the shuttered nightclub. We didn't really have any other choice at that particular point in time, so Rudy and I followed Kenji. I felt my throat tighten with fear as the door to the alley closed behind us, leaving the interior of the nightclub in semidarkness.

From what I could see, it looked like we were in a large room with two pool tables and what might be three strange pinball machines. It was too early for the nightclub to be open yet so the place was dark and silent.

Hiroshi's two thugs hustled us toward the dance floor which was entirely mirrored. Floor, ceiling, walls, everything you can imagine was covered with a mirrored surface. Although there were only five of us, the multitude of our reflections made it seem as though we were in a crowd and believe me, the effect was definitely creepy.

"Over there." The taller bodyguard ushered us toward a catwalk leading upstairs from the dance floor to a narrow balcony overhead. "Let's go," he said curtly, "move it." Kenji and I trudged warily ahead of the two men up the stairs.

"You know, we're not the ones who have been burning down Mr. Saito's businesses in case you're wondering," I spoke up, trying to catch the eye of the shorter bodyguard. "In fact, we've been trying to figure out who has been. This whole thing is probably just a big mistake."

"Yeah, your big mistake, girlie," the shorter guy snapped rudely. It was obvious he wasn't willing to talk things over rationally, so I tried another approach. I closed my eyes briefly, recalling the names of Hiroshi's partners as they had been listed on the articles of incorporation for Saito & Associates, Inc.

"Hey, Saburo!" I spoke sharply. The tall one with the gun glanced up, saying involuntarily, *"Hai?"*

I knew from his reaction that I had correctly guessed his identity and turned to his companion thoughtfully. "All right then. If he's Saburo Watanabe then let's see, that would make you Akira Hamai wouldn't it?" I had clearly unnerved Saburo and Akira. They hadn't expected me to know their full names.

"Shut up, brat," Akira snapped, clenching his hand into a fist. We had reached a mirrored landing at the top of the catwalk now and Saburo ushered us to the end of the balcony until we were facing a door built right into the mirrored wall. Then, Akira reached for the doorknob and opened it inward onto what looked like a small conference room featuring a table at which were seated Hiroshi, Kimiko, Jimmy and Gillian.

14

CAUGHT IN HIROSHI'S TRAP

Hiroshi turned an approving nod on Saburo and Akira as he got to his feet. "Ah, I see our guests are here already. Congratulations. That was quick."

"Found them downstairs in the alleyway," Saburo supplied curtly.

"They were snooping around in the alleyway?"

Hiroshi turned to us with a frown, ordering, "Bring them inside." Akira and Saburo then pushed Kenji, Rudy and me into the room, closing the door after us.

Hiroshi, Kimiko and Gillian were sitting in a semi-circle around the table and they all had plates of food in front of them. A small caterer's wagon stood to one side of the table and it looked as though they had just finished eating.

I looked surreptitiously around, noticing that the decor of the room was similar to the rest of the nightclub. The furnishings were all done in either glass, black leather or stainless steel. The ceiling and three of the walls were mirrored as well, but the fourth wall was made of privacy glass through which you could watch the dance floor below.

"What are *they* doing here?" Kimiko asked, eyeing us doubtfully. "I thought we were all here for an employee meeting, Hiroshi."

"And so we are," Hiroshi reassured her blithely. "Akira, why don't you help our guests find a seat while Kimiko gets us all something to drink."

"*Hai*," Akira replied, then seized Kenji roughly by the arm, pushing him toward a stainless steel and leather chair at the far end of the table. Saburo stood nearby, keeping us covered with the gun, now removed from his pocket, might I add. Jimmy and Gillian exchanged quick glances.

Hiroshi's smile was sinister. "Make sure they can't move around very much, Akira. I need their full attention for our little 'talk'."

I gulped, watching as Akira reached into a cabinet at the far side of the room and produced a roll of duct tape, which he used to strap Kenji's wrists to the sides of his chair. At that point, I must say, things were looking serious indeed, although I had been in worse spots in Mexico in the not-too-distant past.

"Hey!" Kenji protested, trying unsuccessfully to free himself, "what do you think you're doing?"

"Just making sure you don't go anywhere."

Hiroshi smirked. Akira turned and beckoned to Rudy and when Rudy didn't move right away Saburo hefted his gun slightly. Rudy got the message and sat down reluctantly next to Kenji, holding more or less still as his arms were taped to the sides of the chair.

Since I knew better than to challenge the odds against

me I let myself be similarly restrained and found myself sitting closest to Hiroshi, directly beside Kimiko who was at his right. Across the table from us Gillian was watching these proceedings in utter shock, her food entirely forgotten.

"*Omae!*" Hiroshi addressed Kimiko curtly. She shot him a hard little stare, "Yes Hiroshi?"

"Pour us all a drink of sake. Now." Hiroshi didn't say the magic word, nor did Kimiko seem to expect him to. With a shrug, she reached for a bottle of sake on the caterer's cart and I watched as she uncorked it and ceremoniously poured a small cupful of the drink for everyone present.

"*Kampai!*" Hiroshi raised his sake cup enthusiastically but I noticed that Gillian, for one, had a hard time getting into the spirit of the toast. Her eyes looked frightened and she kept giving Kenji, Rudy and me nervous little glances over the rim of her glass.

"*Kampai!*" Hiroshi barked again, and everyone downed their drinks in a toast to everyone else. Everyone except for Hiroshi and Jimmy that is. Since I was sitting closest to Hiroshi I could tell that he had taken no more than the tiniest of sips from his sake cup and the same was true of Jimmy, who pushed his glass away nearly untouched as well.

The moment people had finished their drinks Kimiko poured another yet another round of sake for everyone, refilling their glasses. Hiroshi watched this proceeding with a crazy but indulgent smile, the perfect picture of a genial host gone mad.

Hiroshi pointed at Kenji, giving his receptionist a hard stare. "Now let's get down to business. Gillian, is that the same boy who pretended to be a pizza delivery guy at the office this afternoon, just before the false fire alarm?"

Gillian gulped, looking from Kenji's face to the tape on his wrists. She seemed horrified to be a part of what was happening.

Across the table from me Saburo put his gun down and refilled his glass with more sake from the bottle on the caterer's cart, topping up Akira's glass at the same time.

"That's the boy, I'm pretty sure of it," Gillian replied reluctantly. "I saw the other two children with him right after the fire. They were all leaving the building together."

Nervously, she added, "Mr. Saito, why are they taped up like that? You aren't going to hurt them, are you?"

"Of course I won't hurt them," Hiroshi replied, looking for all the world like a reptile about to swallow some minor prey. "I just want to ask them a few questions about why they broke into my office. I hope you don't object, Gillian." He turned and looked at the three of us.

"Why were you snooping around? Who sent you?" He directed these questions sharply at Kenji who shrugged and replied, "We were delivering a pizza. We had the wrong order."

"You're lying!"

Hiroshi glared at Kenji and crossed the room to stand right in front of him. "You made it look like there was a fire while you broke into my office." His voice was angry and his eyes no more than hard glints in his red face. "Now who sent you? Was it my father?"

"No one sent us. We got the wrong order. And besides, what does your father have to do with this?" Kenji replied, looking blankly back at Hiroshi. Hiroshi lifted a hand and slapped him heavily across the face. Kenji's eyes teared up but he never said a word and I felt a surprising, hot surge of anger well up in me at the way Hiroshi had treated my friend.

"Mr. Saito! What are you *doing?*" Gillian shrieked and stood up, babbling, "I don't want any part of hurting children!"

She seemed nearly hysterical with shock at what she was witnessing. "I really don't think this is *at all* appropriate for an employee meeting!"

"Shut her up," Hiroshi snarled to Akira who put down his sake cup to move around the room in a flash, pushing Gillian far more roughly than necessary back into her chair. She gave him a look of terror then dropped back into her seat without another word. Jimmy eyed Akira with disgust at his rough treatment of Gillian and I saw him shoot her a reassuring little look when Akira's attention was back to Hiroshi.

"How about you? Do you want to talk?" Hiroshi demanded, addressing Rudy.

Rudy gazed back steadfastly. "About what, in particular?"

"You will tell me who sent you!"

"No one sent us, except the pizzeria. What are you talking about, anyway?" At Rudy's answer Hiroshi lifted a hand to smack him too. I saw something in his eyes which told me he would really enjoy hitting my brother and I spoke up quickly. There didn't seem to be any more point in playing games.

"Look, sir, you're making a big mistake! It's true we did break into your office but only because we were trying to find out who's been burning down all of your businesses." I saw Saburo and Akira exchange very odd looks as Hiroshi turned his attention to me.

"Go on." Hiroshi demanded, scowling down at me, his attack on my brother temporarily forgotten.

I gulped then continued, "In case you don't know, the

Murayama's restaurant was burned down this morning just like two of your businesses were. We think that for some reason the arsonist believes there's a connection between you and the Murayama's restaurant. We figured out that Suki's Place will be torched next and came here to see if we could catch whoever has been setting the fires."

"What did you take from my office?"

Kenji answered this question quickly. "We didn't take anything. All we did was look through your files for a list of names of people you've been doing business with to see if one of them is the arsonist."

"Did you tell anyone else what you found?" Hiroshi asked and before either Kenji or Rudy could reply I answered loudly for all three of us. I knew from past experience that there are occasions when a good bluff can be more effective than the unadorned truth. This seemed like just such an occasion.

"We told the police everything we know including all of your names." I nodded at each of them in turn while trying to look calm instead of scared breathless, the way I was actually feeling. "Hiroshi Saito, Gillian Munson, Kimiko Mitsunobu, Akira Hamai, Saburo Watanabe and Jimmy Delapinio."

"How do you know our names?" Gillian broke her silence, casting a quick apprehensive glance at Akira over her shoulder as she spoke.

"They were on the corporate documents we copied in your office, the records for the new company. In fact, we showed those to the police too. Our parents know where we are right now and they're probably calling the police right now." I bluffed, praying that it were true. "So it'll only be a matter of time until the police arrive. If I were you, I'd let us go right now, before you get in bigger trouble.

Kidnapping, forcible detention, those are federal crimes, you know." I could tell I'd struck some kind of a nerve by the way everyone in the room was looking at me.

"New company?" Gillian broke the stillness that followed my words, "What new company? There isn't any new company." I looked her straight in the eyes.

"You mean you don't even know that you're listed as the Secretary Treasurer of Saito & Associates?" She stared blankly back at me.

"I am? What's Saito & Associates?"

"It's a new corporation and you're all equal partners in it. Kimiko is the Accountant, Hiroshi is the—" I would have gone on listing their various corporate titles but just then Akira lurched sideways and leaned heavily against the table with a very strange look on his face.

"I feel... *kimochi warui. Boku wa byoki da yo.*" He looked pale and dizzy, as though he were suddenly feeling light-headed. As we watched, Akira slid down to the floor and sat there leaning against one leg of the table, watching us all in dizzy confusion.

Saburo regarded him at first with amusement, hoisting his sake glass jokingly with a smile which turned slowly to concern as Akira clutched his stomach, whispering, "Aggghh," or something like that. I didn't quite catch the Japanese.

Saburo got up and went over to help him. "You all right, man?" Saburo looked wildly across the room at Hiroshi. "Hey boss, there's something wrong with him, we better call—" Saburo paused, and an odd look crossed his face too. "Uhh," he whispered faintly, "I don't feel very good either." He toppled over to sprawl motionlessly beside Akira, his gun falling loosely from his fingers onto the floor.

"What's going on? Why do I feel so funny?" Kimiko's voice sounded shrill and she looked impatiently around the room, as though waiting for someone to answer her question. Hiroshi merely raised his eyebrows at her in an exaggerated expression of puzzlement as Gillian too shook her head woozily. Jimmy turned a stunned look on Gillian as she clutched desperately at his sleeve.

"Something's the matter with me," she whispered to him in a frightened voice, her eyes going accusingly toward Hiroshi. "Call a doctor," Gillian murmured weakly, just before she passed out.

Beside me, Kimiko moaned and collapsed forward across the table, looking like she had had too much to drink. Only Hiroshi and Jimmy seemed unaffected by the strange illness which was afflicting the others.

"What's going on here?" Jimmy demanded. He looked uneasy as he got to his feet and looked around at the unconscious forms of his fellow employees. Hiroshi got to his feet as well, and I saw him eye Jimmy's untouched sake cup.

"I think it's probably food poisoning, or something," Hiroshi answered smoothly, "the caterers must have messed up."

"Looks like it," Jimmy said slowly, feeling for a pulse in Gillian's neck. "I'm calling a doctor."

"Good idea, but first let's have a drink!" Hiroshi proposed, lifting his glass in a toast. Jimmy stared back at him, mystified by this unexpected and utterly inappropriate invitation.

"Ah, that's all right, I'll pass." Jimmy gave him an odd look. "You go ahead without me boss, I'm calling the doctor."

"Please, join me," Hiroshi said a little more firmly, sliding the sake cup across the table toward Jimmy.

"I don't think so." Jimmy shook his head, backing away.

"I insist," Hiroshi snarled and Jimmy's eyebrows flew up in surprise. But Jimmy's look of surprise quickly turned to one of wariness and he looked at the cup of sake before him as though seeing it for the first time.

"Don't drink it Jimmy," I spoke up suddenly, "I bet Hiroshi put something in the sake and poisoned everyone. He probably even tried to poison you too. See? You two are the only ones who haven't had any sake to drink." That was as far as I got, because Hiroshi strode forward and hit me hard across the face.

"Stop lying girlie." he said, or at least that's what I think he said. I really couldn't tell since my ears were sort of ringing for a second or two after that.

"Leave her alone, you freakin' ape!" Rudy was furious. "Are you all right K.C?"

I nodded gingerly as the feeling returned to the side of my face.

"She's lying, it's obviously food poisoning." Hiroshi turned smoothly back to Jimmy, all smiles.

"Right," Jimmy replied, but I saw his gaze travel from his own cup of sake to Hiroshi's untouched cup then to the empty cups of the others as Hiroshi continued, "But enough about drinking. I think you're right, Jimmy. Our friends need medical attention right away so why don't you go ahead and call the doctor." Hiroshi gestured at the telephone on the wall across the room and Jimmy licked his lips, glancing nervously at the open door then back at Hiroshi. I wasn't at all surprised that he wanted to leave the room.

"Well?" Hiroshi prompted, still smiling. "Go ahead, make the call. You can use the phone over there."

"Well the thing is, you see I just remembered something I forgot downstairs," Jimmy was edging carefully toward the door as he spoke, the travesty of nonchalance in his voice. "I'll be right back."

"Fine," Hiroshi smiled agreeably, "no problem Jimmy." His words sounded sincere, but still Jimmy hesitated, his eyes darting nervously from the door to Hiroshi's face then back again.

"Right," he said again and headed quickly for the door. He might have made it out of the room unharmed if he hadn't turned his back on Hiroshi for a split second.

Hiroshi stooped quickly to pick up Saburo's gun, lifting and pointing it right at Jimmy's back. There was the roar of a shot and Jimmy went down, falling in a motionless heap across the doorway. It looked like he was dead, and I knew without a doubt then that Hiroshi planned to kill us all.

15

SAY YOUR PRAYERS

There was silence in the room for a moment as Rudy, Kenji and I all stared at each other in silence. Their faces were as white as mine. There was no need for any exchange of words to express what we all felt.

We watched, stunned as Hiroshi tucked Saburo's gun into his jacket pocket then looted his fallen employees, quickly removing the cash and jewellery from their wallets, persons and purses one by one.

"I don't get it," Kenji said finally. "Why would you want to kill your own employees? Are they the ones who have been burning down your businesses?"

"Of course not, you idiot," Hiroshi sneered contemptuously.

Kenji persisted. "Then why?"

"Why should I tell you kids anything?" Hiroshi replied curtly.

"Why not tell us? You're planning to kill us all anyway, aren't you?" Kenji retorted. Hiroshi smiled a twisted little smile, nodding smugly. I felt the skin all along my neck prickle as he replied, cool as a cucumber, "You're right about that part."

"But why?" Rudy protested. "Why would you want to kill us? We're not the ones who started all those fires!"

"I know." Hiroshi grunted.

"Then what have you got against us?"

"You know too much," he replied shortly, "so now you have to die too."

"We *know* too much?" Kenji sounded confused and outraged. "What are you talking about? We don't even know who's been setting all the fires! How can we know too much?" Instead of answering, Hiroshi got to his feet and crossed the room, standing over Jimmy where he lay blocking the door.

Jimmy had fallen so that he was blocking the exit and Hiroshi stooped, dragging him by the feet to one side so that the door was clear. Jimmy wasn't a very heavy man, but even so Hiroshi panted a little with the strain of his exertions and by the time he had hauled Jimmy feet-first back inside the room Hiroshi was looking flushed and a little winded.

Hiroshi carelessly removed his own jacket and slung it over the back of Kimiko's chair beside me, wiping his forehead as he checked to be sure that Rudy, Kenji and I were all still securely taped to our chairs.

"I'm going out for a minute. Don't even think of trying anything funny, and don't bother screaming because these walls are soundproof," he told us. The minute Hiroshi left the room Kenji and Rudy turned to me, their expressions urgent.

"Now's our chance!"

"K.C., get the gun!" They spoke simultaneously and I

realized that Hiroshi had accidentally left Saburo's gun behind. It was still in the side pocket of his jacket which he'd draped over Kimiko's chair. Since I was closest, I had the best chance of success of getting to it first.

I scooted my stainless steel chair sideways across the thick carpet as quickly as I could, straining with my fingers to reach the gun tucked into the pocket of Hiroshi's jacket. The tape restraining my hand just barely allowed me to touch the gun.

"I can just barely grasp it," I whispered to Rudy and Kenji in frustration, "but I won't be able to point it at him."

"Then just jam it or something!" Kenji whispered.

"How?" I hissed back, frustrated by my lack of knowledge about the unfamiliar handgun.

"It looks to me like a semiautomatic," Kenji replied quietly. "Put your fingers on the grip of the gun, the part where you hold it and feel for a little button on the inside. Do you feel it?" I nodded, glancing nervously at the stairs. In the distance I could hear Hiroshi clattering back up the catwalk toward us and I knew I didn't have much time.

"Push the button," Kenji continued, "it'll eject the ammunition." I followed Kenji's instructions and a cylinder of metal popped out of the gun's handle into my palm. After fumbling for a moment I was able to drop the ammunition clip onto the floor at my feet where I kicked it away as far as I could with my toe. I left the gun itself in Hiroshi's jacket.

"Good job, K.C.," Kenji whispered, "that means there's only one bullet left, the one in the chamber."

"'Only' one?" I repeated, chagrined. 'Only one' bullet was more than enough to do some pretty serious damage to a person, after all. Hiroshi's return put an end to our conversation and the three of us fell silent as he rejoined us.

He was carrying two big, bright-red, metal gasoline cans and was wearing gloves with some sort of apron tied over his suit. I got the impression he was dressed for a barbecue and then felt myself turn pale as I realized that if he was the cook, we were....

"Wait a minute," I addressed Hiroshi, watching with growing apprehension as he unscrewed the cap of one of the cans and began pouring gasoline in a trail around the room. "You're not worried about who's been starting all the fires because you already know who the arsonist is. It was you the whole time, wasn't it?" Hiroshi grunted a little as he splashed gasoline in a wide arc around the room, making sure that his employees were all thoroughly drenched with the stuff.

"It was me," he admitted finally. "Fires have always been a little hobby of mine. Different things burn in different ways, did you know that?" I blinked at his words as Hiroshi went on. "Take this room for instance. It looks almost fireproof, but once the glass on the walls shatter, believe me the insulation inside will burn quite well. Not everyone knows that," he added with a touch of pride, "but like I said, fires are a little hobby of mine." Hiroshi seemed very proud of himself.

"Did you burn down our restaurant too?" Kenji asked, to which Hiroshi replied by a smirk and a shrug.

"Sure, that was me. Good job, too"

"Why? My father's restaurant has nothing to do with you. What have you got against us?" At Kenji's words, Hiroshi spat sideways onto the floor.

"Your 'precious' father and I go back a long way. Didn't he tell you he worked for the Yakuza when he was younger?" Kenji's eyes flickered as Hiroshi went on, "It was many years ago, but I knew your father when he was nothing. Worse than scum. He owes everything he has now to me."

With these words Hiroshi tossed the empty can of gasoline aside and reached for the second can, unscrewing the lid as he favored us with an evil smile.

"But why are you burning everything down?" I asked quickly, trying to keep him talking. "Is this all some sort of insurance scam? You know that won't work, right? I mean, everyone knows that most insurance policies won't pay off on cases of obvious arson."

"That's right," Kenji put in, "so if that's why you're doing all this you might as well let us go because it won't work. Even you can't be stupid enough to think it would." Hiroshi's gloating smile faded abruptly as he grasped the implications of Kenji's remark.

"Worm, you dare to call me stupid?"

Hiroshi put the gas can down carefully, his hands clenching and unclenching as he stepped closer to Kenji.

"Shut up!" he shouted, his face turning a deep purple in color as he wrenched Saburo's gun from his pocket and pointed it right at Kenji. "You're wrong about me! I am not stupid! Don't call me stupid!! It's not my fault if I'm unlucky! You take that back!" Hiroshi's hands were trembling violently on the trigger and I spoke up, trying to keep my own voice from shaking as I tried to soothe him.

"All right, all right, please calm down Mr. Saito. Kenji didn't mean what he said. You're a genius master criminal and your plan is very, very good.

"I'm sorry." Kenji muttered after a moment, "I'm sorry I called you an idiot. You're a brilliant master criminal, I guess I just didn't see it before."

He repeated these words in a mutinous monotone, but Hiroshi seemed to take them at face value and put Saburo's gun back in his pocket with a nod, his injured pride apparently appeased.

"Shooting is too good for you anyway," Hiroshi said with a smile. I shuddered, knowing full well that he meant to burn us alive. My only hope was to keep him talking long enough for Darrell and Trina to find us before he could light the blaze.

"I still don't see why you would want to kill your own employees though." I spoke conversationally, "I mean, none of this makes any sense unless...." I trailed off, staring at him in growing horror. "Wait a minute." I was remembering Gillian's reaction when I'd mentioned Saito & Associates. "There's something else going on, something to do with that new company of yours, Saito & Associates. You're planning to murder them all for their life insurance policies aren't you?" I guessed and Hiroshi threw me a quick, annoyed look over his shoulder.

"Five dead business partners, five million dollars," Hiroshi broke his silence, confirming my guess. "And to think they say it's hard to find valuable employees these days!" he paused to let us appreciate his sense of humor and then continued, "too bad you kids had to go poking around where you didn't belong."

I couldn't help gasping when Hiroshi began sloshing gasoline on Kenji, Rudy and me one by one. He took special pleasure in pouring the stuff on me, smiling broadly when some accidentally splashed on my face. I tried to ignore the fact that I had just become highly flammable and tried to be cool about the whole situation but it was hard.

"Listen to me, Hiroshi!" Kenji protested with ill-concealed frustration, "what you're planning to do here won't work either. You obviously lied on their life insurance applications and when the insurance company finds out about that they'll never pay off! You're wasting your time, don't you see? This is all really pointless!"

"Who says they'll find out?" Hiroshi asked reasonably. "Who will tell them differently?"

"Listen to me. None of the insurance companies are going to pay off. The mere fact that there have been so many arson incidents in town lately makes it impossible that they'll believe this is all an accident. They'll investigate and when they do, they'll find out that Jimmy here was killed by a gunshot. They won't pay off for months, maybe years, if ever. Don't you get it?! How can you be so stu.." I shot Kenji a warning look and he stopped himself in mid-word. After that we all watched silently as Hiroshi tossed the second empty gas can aside and reached for his jacket, shrugging it on.

Patting his jacket pocket to make sure Saburo's gun was still there Hiroshi stepped over the fallen bodies of his comrades, admiring his own handiwork with a great deal of satisfaction.

"Oh come on man. Think about it." Kenji tried futilely one last time to talk Hiroshi out of what he planned to do. "This can't work. You have to see that. You *do* see that, don't you?" Hiroshi ignored Kenji's words, humming a little as he crossed the room.

He stopped at the door and Kenji, Rudy and I watched in absolute dread as he proceeded to search his pockets at length, looking here and there for something that eluded him. Finally he produced a cigarette lighter and held it triumphantly aloft.

"Say your prayers, you little brats." My heart raced with terror as Hiroshi smiled and flicked the lighter.

16

A FATHER'S CURSE

But nothing happened. There was no spark, no flame whatsoever. Hiroshi flicked the lighter again then again.

With a muttered curse, he redoubled his efforts, flicking the lighter over and over and despite our predicament Kenji and I exchanged tiny smiles when he finally lost his temper and hurled the useless lighter across the room with a shout of rage.

Still muttering under his breath, Hiroshi crouched over his unconscious employees, searching them one by one for another lighter or a book of matches. Needless to say he was livid when he failed to find anything of the sort on his victims.

"Stay right there!" Hiroshi ordered us harshly, and since we were unable to move, completely uselessly. Then he left the room. A moment later, we heard his feet clattering down the catwalk. I had a sinking feeling that he was heading for the bar downstairs and I just knew he would easily find a supply of matches there.

Kenji was tugging frantically at the tape on his wrists. "Oh man! Can you believe this guy? What are we going to do now?"

"Maybe there's something over here we can use to cut ourselves free," I said, and rocked my chair over toward the caterer's table. But there were no knives amid the assortment of plastic cutlery assembled there. "Nope, nothing here is sharp enough."

"Maybe we can wake one of these guys up to help us," Rudy suggested, sliding his chair around so that he could give Akira a vicious poke with his foot. "Hey Akira! Can you hear me? You have to wake up!" Akira moaned and mumbled a little but didn't awaken even though Rudy redoubled his efforts.

Eventually I remarked, "Stop it Rudy it's no use. He's totally unconscious. You're just going to break his ribs or something if you keep that up."

"Serve him right if I did, anyway," Rudy muttered but ceased his attack on Akira's torso.

"Shhh," Kenji cautioned us. "He's coming back."

"This is it, then," Rudy whispered grimly squaring his shoulders. "I just want you both two to know I'm sorry it all has to end this way."

"Hey, knock it off! It's not over yet," Kenji objected "Remember, it isn't over until the fat lady sings!" He was joking bravely, trying to cheer us up, but I didn't get the reference.

"What fat lady?"

"As in the opera," Kenji explained a little impatiently. "A lot of the sopranos are, well—oh, never mind. It's just a stupid saying."

"Sayonara, little brats!" we heard Hiroshi's evil chuckle outside the room.

"That sounds like her singing now," I remarked hopelessly as he rounded the corner with a book of matches from the restaurant downstairs clutched in his chubby fist. He stood in the doorway and tore one of the matches off, lifting it to strike against the rough sandpaper edge of the matchbook.

Time seemed to stand still. I felt my focus narrow to anticipate the moment when the first spark would leap from the matchbook. Then suddenly, amazingly, someone else spoke. Someone who must have been standing behind Hiroshi on the balcony.

"I would not do that if I were you, Hiroshi."

I recognized Mr. Murayama's voice immediately, as did Kenji.

"Dad!" he shouted urgently, "Watch out! He has a gun!" Hiroshi turned with the match in his hand still poised for striking as Mr. Murayama stepped into view. He was unarmed but there was something fearless and hard about the way he confronted Hiroshi.

Without a word, Hiroshi dropped the matchbook on the floor and grabbed for Saburo's gun but Mr. Murayama was way too fast for him. He moved across the distance separating them so quickly that Hiroshi had no chance to defend himself against the wicked karate chop Mr. Murayama applied to his face.

Hiroshi went staggering backwards, firing the only bullet in Saburo's gun harmlessly into the floor. Mr. Murayama crouched, readying himself for another attack and when Hiroshi raised and pointed the gun at him again Mr. Murayama rolled under the table toward Hiroshi, employing a stunning side kick to Hiroshi's midriff from the floor near his feet. The gun went flying from Hiroshi's hand as he doubled over, clutching his gut.

"You—" Hiroshi wheezed and gasped helplessly for air, leaning against the wall for support, which gave Mr. Murayama a chance to glance at Kenji, Rudy and me.

"Are you kids all right?"

We nodded silently as he got to his feet. I was more than all right. I was more relieved than I'd ever been in my whole life. Well, for a while, anyway, as you'd know if you have been reading my other travel diaries.

But Hiroshi wasn't finished. When he thought Mr. Murayama wasn't watching him, he made his move. The gun was too far away for him to reach as he lunged for the bottle of sake on the caterer's cart and swung it aloft, obviously intending to break it over Mr. Murayama's head in true Hollywood fashion. Unfortunately for Hiroshi, the bottle was uncorked and since he was holding it by the neck all of the sake inside came gurgling down his wrist, soaking into the sleeve of his pale violet suit.

With a scream of rage, Hiroshi threw the bottle at Mr. Murayama, but he easily ducked, and there was an amazing explosion of glass as the bottle hit and shattered the mirrored wall at the far end of the room.

"That's enough, *omae*." A stranger's deep voice interrupted this little tableau and I looked up in surprise to see that a very old Japanese man had arrived unnoticed during the fuss and was standing in the doorway of the room. Even though it wasn't open for business yet, Suki's Place had turned out to be quite the popular gathering spot.

Mr. Murayama straightened slowly from his defensive crouch to stand warily facing the old man. He and the other man measured each other with their eyes intent. "Tadao Saito," Mr. Murayama said.

Hiroshi stared at the newcomer, his face pale with shock. *"Oyabun,"* Hiroshi whispered finally, "What brings you here?"

* * *

FLASHBACK

Tokyo, Japan, nine months before the present day. In a tall office building in downtown Shinjuku, Hiroshi Saito sits sullenly in front of his father's polished, mahogany desk.

It is nearly twenty years since we have last seen Hiroshi and the years have not been kind to him. He has softened and thickened considerably and the lines of his face have settled into a permanently displeased pout, while the shape of his body has long since succumbed to gravity.

Hiroshi is slouching in a comfortable black leather chair, his shoulders hunched in shame at his latest failure. While getting drunk at a local karaoke bar, he has inadvertently provided an undercover policeman with enough evidence to close down two out of three of Tadao Saito's operations in Kyoto, a city south of Tokyo. Since the project in Kyoto has taken several years for him to establish, Tadao Saito is particularly displeased with its premature failure.

This disaster is only the most recent in Hiroshi's troubled history as a Yakuza member. Over the years, Hiroshi has gotten into serious trouble with loan sharks over gambling debts, bumbled himself in and out of jail several times for attacking women in hostess clubs and generally led a life of absolute dissipation. In fact, the only thing he has achieved over the last twenty years is to become an accomplished liar and cheat, a disgrace to his father's carefully planned operations.

Tadao Saito stands across the room, staring down from huge picture windows at the sprawling city below. The office building itself is tall enough to clear the slight layer of haze which blankets modern day Tokyo, and Tadao Saito can see blue sky from his vantage point.

"You have disgraced this family. You disgrace me. You disgrace yourself."

Tadao Saito speaks with finality as he turns to face his son. He drops the bland mask he usually presents to the world, showing his only son the true face of his anger. "You are leaving Tokyo, *omae*, and you will not come back."

Hiroshi opens his mouth to protest, but Tadao Saito continues speaking. His voice is controlled even though his eyes blaze with anger.

"This is your very last chance. You will oversee a small new business enterprise of mine, nothing very difficult, of course," he adds sarcastically. "I am opening up a mahjong parlor, a danceteria and a hostess bar on the island of Maui, in Hawaii. All I ask is that you report to me on their progress and stay out of trouble. If you fail this too, if you make even one more mistake, there will be no place for you in my house ever again."

Hiroshi's eyes widen at this threat. Although the words themselves mean little, Tadao Saito's use of the word 'house' is all-encompassing and represents the world of the Yakuza. Hiroshi understands that he is close to being banished from the Yakuza entirely and he knows that, without his father's protection, any one of the dozens of enemies he has made over the years will gladly help speed his death.

"Maui?" Hiroshi croaks finally, attempting a smile. Hiroshi has always blamed others for his own shortcomings and he sees his father's decree as an insult to his own pride, rather than recognizing the mercy he is actually being shown. Although his face is carefully blank, Hiroshi is seething with fury inside. "Maui sounds good. Lots of pretty women." Hiroshi's lips stretch painfully tight across his lips but he keeps smiling anyway. It is very difficult for him to contain the rage he feels at being exiled to Maui but he can see that his father's patience is nearly exhausted.

At Hiroshi's reference to pretty women Tadao Saito's eyes narrow and his nostrils flare in disgust. He is thinking of the assault charges recently filed against Hiroshi by a formerly lovely girl working at a local hostess bar.

Tadao Saito walks deliberately across the room and leans over his son. Although he is standing still, there is an air of extreme menace about him. Hiroshi cowers slightly before the old man's quiet wrath.

Tadao speaks deliberately, explicitly communicating his meaning with words and thereby insulting Hiroshi's intelligence, "Just so you understand. If you get into trouble on Maui, any trouble at all, you will be finished in this family, forever. Do you understand me? *Wakaru?*"

"*Hai, wakaru,*" Hiroshi mumbles and lowers his eyes so that his father cannot see the humiliated fury burning in them.

"Good. I have arranged for you to leave tomorrow." Without even saying goodbye Tadao Saito leaves the room. As his father passes him, Hiroshi leaps to his feet and bows low, as humbly as possible. Then, once his father has left the room, Hiroshi drops his pose and makes a rude gesture at the closed door. "Treat me like a child will you?" he snarls, "You'll be sorry for that, you old fool!"

* * *

The man Mr. Murayama had called Tadao Saito stepped into the room without answering Hiroshi's question, looking around thoughtfully. Despite the fact that he was gazing upon a scene which included five motionless people sprawling in a pool of gasoline, three kids taped to chairs and two grown men engaged in a life and death battle, his expression was entirely blank. He could have been looking at a sunset. I felt a chill as his eyes met and went right through mine.

"What are you doing here, father?" Hiroshi repeated nervously, once he had regained his breath enough to speak coherently.

Without answering Hiroshi, Tadao Saito gestured behind himself to someone else and another man dressed in black shirt and slacks followed him into the room. At the sight of the other man, Hiroshi's face paled even more and he started to back away.

"Jun, cut them free." Tadao Saito motioned the newcomer with a curt gesture to the three of us. To my intense relief the man he'd called Jun strode forward and cut the tape from my wrists, turning to do the same for Kenji and Rudy. We stood up and rubbed our wrists thankfully as Mr. Murayama crossed quickly to Kenji's side, assuring himself of his son's well-being.

"So what brings you here, father?" Hiroshi repeated, trying for a nonchalant tone of voice but failing miserably.

"I am here because of the strange rumors I've been hearing about my operations here on Maui," Tadao Saito told him softly, "and because of an interesting phone conversation I had with my old friend, Masataka Murayama, some hours ago. But let us speak first of what has been happening here."

His tone became, if anything even more gentle, but like a tiger toying with its prey. Although his words weren't exactly a question, it was crystal clear that he was awaiting Hiroshi's immediate explanation.

"Here?" Hiroshi raised his eyebrows, clearly stalling for time. "You mean in this room?" he licked his lips. "All right. It was like this: These children are responsible for everything. I caught them in the act of trying to burn down the nightclub and taped them to the chairs to restrain them."

This was a pitiful story and I saw Jun glance at Tadao Saito for a split second then look away, his face a carefully controlled mask.

"Sorry, that's not true," I cheerfully put in. "Hiroshi was going to kill everyone in here for their life insurance money. He's the one who's been burning down all of your other businesses, too. He told us so himself." Tadao Saito turned his piercing gaze from me back to Hiroshi.

"It's a lie, father!" Hiroshi protested wildly. "These children are the ones who started the fires, I tell you. I had just finished capturing them when Masataka arrived and attacked me!" He couldn't quite meet his father's eyes as he uttered this preposterous lie and an embarrassed pause followed his words.

"You are lying to me again, *Omae.*" Tadao Saito shook his head. "I gave you one last chance to succeed on Maui, and even here you have failed and shamed me."

Hiroshi gamely tried to talk his way out of the mess he'd made but there was real fear in his eyes as he faced his father. "I can explain everything. None of this is my fault!"

Tadao Saito ignored his son's protest and continued, "I warned you not to make any more mistakes and instead you have sabotaged my business on Maui. In the past, I have forgiven you because you are my son and because you are not very bright but this time there can be no special treatment."

Hiroshi flushed beet red with embarrassment at this unflattering description of his intellect and abilities. "You've got it all wrong!" he protested. "I swear the children started the fires!" Hiroshi was babbling in sheer terror by now and edging around the table as he spoke. Suddenly, he dove in desperation for the floor, grabbing at something out of sight. When he got up he was clutching Saburo's gun. Hiroshi pointed the weapon triumphantly at his father. "Sop. One move and you die, old fool! I'm leaving and nobody better try to stop me!"

Tadao Saito's eyes narrowed at his son's daring bid for

freedom. "Put the gun down. Now." He sounded more weary than alarmed.

Out of the corner of my, eye I saw Jun shift ever so slightly and Hiroshi turned on him instantly.

"Don't move!" Jun froze.

"You cannot succeed, Hiroshi. Put the gun down."

Hiroshi snickered rudely, "You think you can still push me around?" You doddering old man, can't you see I'm the one in control now? Do you think I won't kill you? Well, you're wrong. I'll kill you right here! I'll wipe out every trace of your organization here on Maui and then I'll be the one in charge!"

"Is that what you think? That when I am gone you will be the one in charge?" Tadao Saito shook his head sadly, nonplussed for the first time since he had walked into the room. "Put down the gun and stop being such a fool."

"You dare to call me a fool?" Hiroshi's voice grew angrier as he realized his father wasn't afraid of him. "You've always underestimated me, called me stupid. Well you'll pay for that, old man. I'm going to shoot you right here and now."

Kenji suddenly spoke up. "There's just one problem, Hiroshi. That gun you're holding isn't loaded. We took all the bullets out."

"You're just trying to trick me." Hiroshi snarled

"'Fraid not, Hiroshi," I smiled. "I took the clip out myself. You left the jacket with the gun inside here in the room with us when you left. Remember? Then you used the last bullet in the chamber to shoot at Kenji's father. That gun is empty." Hiroshi raised the gun anyway, aiming it, point blank, at his father's head.

"Oh yeah? Let's see," he said, pulling the trigger. When nothing happened, Hiroshi's triumphant expression changed to one of utter terror and he flung the gun from him with a curse and sprinted for the door. Tadao Saito sighed heavily then glanced at Jun, his eyes narrowing with disgust.

"Bring him back," he ordered. Jun pulled out his own gun then followed Hiroshi quickly down the balcony. After a moment we heard a tremendous crash followed by Hiroshi's voice whimpering for mercy. Through the one-way glass window overlooking the dance floor, I was able to see that Jun had Hiroshi pinned to the dance floor below us. Things were definitely starting to look up.

"I apologize for my son," Tadao Saito said quite formally to Mr. Murayama, Kenji, Rudy and me. "He has dishonored our family. Now please come, let's leave this room." He led us all out onto the balcony and although I was glad to leave the gas fumes behind I couldn't help worrying a little about Gillian and the others.

"What about them?" I asked gesturing behind us at the unconscious forms of Hiroshi's erstwhile employees. I had seen Gillian's chest rising and falling as though she slept so I knew that the drug Hiroshi had given his employees wasn't fatal.

"I will see that they quickly receive proper medical treatment," Tadao Saito replied calmly as we took the catwalk downstairs to the dance floor where Jun had handcuffed Hiroshi to a trashcan. Bruised and clearly humiliated, he stood before his father with his head bowed.

Just then, the back door to Suki's Place literally burst open and we all whirled around to find ourselves facing three armed security guards led by Darrell.

17

RESCUED

Darrell took the situation in at a glance, his eyes meeting mine warily. "K.C., Rudy, you all right?"

I saw Jun tense, glancing at Tadao Saito, so I replied quickly, "Everything's okay, Darrell. This is Mr. Saito. He's Hiroshi's father. He and Kenji's father just saved us from Hiroshi."

"It is just as K.C. tells you. The situation is under control," Mr. Murayama reassured him. Darrell's brow crinkled a little but he nodded and the men with him relaxed.

"This is an old acquaintance of mine, Tadao Saito. Saito-san, please meet Darrell Hughes." The two men shook hands carefully after Mr. Murayama introduced them. "Saito-san has been helping us sort out the misunderstanding between Hiroshi and the kids," Mr. Murayama finished — a strange way of putting it, I thought — and I saw Darrell give him an odd look of comprehension.

"A misunderstanding. I see." He turned to study Hiroshi with open hatred. "Is there anything I can do to help?" he asked, turning back to Mr. Murayama, then sniffed the air., "Smells like someone has a gas leak in here. Is that gasoline on your clothes, kids?"

"It's a very long story," I told him drily, and Darrell's eyes narrowed.

"I can see that K.C. but what I need to know is—."

"I am sorry for any harm my son has caused your children," Tadao Saito interjected, as he bowed deeply to Darrell. "Please accept my apologies. I am in your debt and I would be privileged to have an opportunity to repay you in the future."

"Thanks for helping the kids, Mr. Saito," Darrell replied, warming to the old man, "but the way I see it we're square."

"Square?" Tadao Saito looked puzzled.

Darrell tried to explain. "It means we're even, as in you don't owe me anything."

Tadao Saito nodded politely. "I see. And now I will take care of the situation here. There is no need for any of you to trouble yourselves further over what has happened tonight." Although his words were gracious it was clear that Hiroshi's father was politely inviting us all to hit the road.

"Thank you for your help," Mr. Murayama bowed to him deeply and then the four of us left the conference room without looking back. All right, I confess I did take one last peek over my shoulder as I left the room and it did me a world of good to see the look on Tadao Saito's face. Hiroshi would undoubtedly get what he had coming to him.

It was nearly midnight by the time we all got home to Trina. We stopped on the way home to call her and tell her we were all right but she was still pretty frantic with worry by the time we reached the house and ran for the showers to get the smell of gasoline off.

When we emerged, feeling better and looking more human again, Mr. Murayama was still talking to mom and Darrell, explaining what had transpired. Then it was our turn. When we were all through a first round of talking, Trina let Rudy and me know exactly what she thought about kids who disobeyed direct orders and went out snooping around Yakuza nightclubs after dark. For once she directed the majority of her reprimands at my older brother. I have to admit it kind of did my soul good to see Rudy take a turn in the hotseat.

Trina did calm down eventually, as parents always do. After all, none of us was actually hurt, except maybe for our clothes which were fit only for the garbage after being so thoroughly soaked with gasoline. Rudy had lent Kenji some clothes, which let mom make a sappy comment about having an extra son in the house. Then she served a plateful of sandwiches for snacks. It's true, food really does calm the beasts, as they say! We ate while I (now it was MY turn, K.C. Flanagan, girl detective reports to her commanding officers. Yeah!) added all the details our parental units wanted, filling in mom, Darrell and Mr. Murayama on everything that had transpired before the endgame at the club.

"So, what you're saying, now, is that Hiroshi was burning down all of his father's businesses out of revenge for the way his father had treated him." Mr. Murayama nodded at Darrell's summary of our findings.

"More or less. He was planning to take over the Yakuza operations here on Maui, using the money from the life insurance policies on his partners."

"Lucky for us, he didn't plan very well," Trina commented, smiling a little in spite of herself.

"Lucky for us he's an idiot," Kenji added happily,

polishing off his second sandwich and reaching for another one. "Mrs. Flanagan—"

"Gigantes, Kenji, pronounced like 'Atlantis,' and soon to be Gigantes-Hughes," mom added, looking ever the sly fox while revealing the secret she had obviously been itching to tell us. "Darrell and I have set a date for our marriage."

Boy! This evening was just one long roller-coaster ride. I jumped over to hug her and Darrell, as did Rudy. Kenji and his father warmly shook their hands.

But there were still a couple of loose ends in the Hiroshi business to discuss. I asked, to no one in particular, "Do you think his plan could ever have worked, though? I mean if we hadn't interfered?"

Darrell shook his head. "Probably not, K.C. Corporate life insurance policies can be pretty tricky and since Hiroshi lied about his partners when he applied for the insurance policies, chances are they would never have paid off."

"Hiroshi was always quite foolish," Mr. Murayama put in quietly. Kenji gave his father a quick look as Mr. Murayama continued, "But then I, too, have done some foolish things in my life." He finished quietly. "A long time ago, when I was a young man in my twenties, I worked for the Yakuza."

Darrell's eyes narrowed with interest at this new information. "Oh?"

"But I put that part of my life behind me many years ago," Mr. Murayama smiled obliquely, "and now I am just a humble sushi chef."

Trina immediately jumped in, saying, "Oh, but Mr. Murayama, your sushi is not humble at all. Your creations are really high sushi art."

That broke the tension, and then Kenji said, "Huh," eyeing his father respectfully. "I want to hear the whole story now and from the beginning."

Masataka Murayama smiled at his son. "Maybe someday, son, maybe someday," he promised, as he turned to us and said, "Now, please, dear friends, you must excuse Kenji and me. This has been a very eventful, but tiring evening. We must sleep and then begin to plan the rebuilding of our restaurant. Lucky for us, the bonsai garden was not ruined by the fire. So we will make it the center of the new Sushi Ya. Perhaps it will bring us clients who are more interested in art and less in arson."

With that, our friends turned and left us to celebrating the upcoming wedding.

EPILOGUE

Kenji wrote to Rudy and me from Hawaii a few weeks after we went home to Montreal, to tell us the KoSa Kaisha, Inc. had closed its doors completely, shutting down its business operations on Maui and gone elsewhere. All that remains of the Saito legacy in Lahaina these days are a few charred buildings and some 'for rent' signs.

Kenji and his father were able to rebuild their restaurant within a month of our departure from Maui. According to Kenji, a mysterious business partner stepped in not long after their restaurant burned down to give the Murayamas a hand with financing the reconstruction. Kenji never said so, but I suspect it was Tadao Saito who helped them. Kenji also sent us a clipping from The Maui News which read something like this:

Car Crash Injures One

Late last night, a local businessman was involved in a single-car accident. The driver apparently fell asleep at the wheel and lost control of his vehicle. Authorities say the driver, who suffered severe head injuries and is currently in intensive care, has been identified as Hiroshi Saito, age 44, of Lahaina. Police have ruled the crash an accident."

Hiroshi never did quite recover from his head injuries. In fact, the last I heard he was quite happily learning how to weave bamboo place mats in a care facility on Honolulu not far from where KoSa Kaisha, Inc. now runs its businesses.

Gillian, Kimiko, Saburo and Akira made a nice recovery from Hiroshi's poisoning attempt at the local hospital but I never heard what happened to Jimmy and whether he lived or died. Kenji didn't either. When I asked him, he told me that there was nothing in the papers about it. It was like Jimmy had just disappeared off the face of the earth.

I don't know why Gillian, Kimiko and the others never went public with their story. Maybe Tadao Saito found some way to 'encourage' them not to talk. In any event, the local press only gave the fire at Suki's Place a few paragraphs then dropped the topic forever.

To the best of my knowledge, the mystery of the arson in Lahaina was never officially solved. Kenji told us that, once the fires stopped, the police (for lack of any further evidence) closed their file on the arson investigation and closed it remains, seemingly, to this day.

Rudy and I did ask Father whether or not we should tell the authorities all we knew, but he advised us against it since we had no real evidence to prove that what we had witnessed had actually happened. And besides, a kind of justice had been done. Ultimately, it seemed wisest just to leave the whole thing alone. So that's what we did.

All in all, once we finally got Hiroshi out of the way, I had a great time on Maui. I learned how to snorkel and dive with the best of them and even got a super tan from lying around on the beach reading books. We went to the top of Mt. Haleakala, a stunning experience which stayed with me for days, and Trina's exhibition almost sold out entirely.

She got rave reviews from the local critics and several offers from Galleries around the world to show her next series of glass works. (I doubt she'll be working in glass for a while, though, since she ordered a big block of marble by phone before we left Maui for a stretch in Dallas. Darrell tells me she has been sketching up a storm in her studio down there.)

I learned a lot about myself on Maui, too. I had started my vacation with the firm resolve to avoid trouble. Yet trouble had found me anyway. Maybe it was luck, or maybe fate. After a few days of lying around in the sun pondering pre-destiny, I decided I might as well just accept who I am and learn to live my life as me.

So just for the record, I'm back home in Montreal, and officially back in the detecting business again. In fact, I'm even thinking about getting some business cards printed up and starting my own private detective agency. I could do that! 'K.C. Flanagan, girl detective. No job too large or too small. International experience.' Sounds nice to my ears!

Rudy and Kenji still talk all the time on the internet. In fact, this morning, I heard Rudy asking Father if Kenji could come to stay with us for a week. Kenji has never seen snow, and if there is one thing we have lots of in this place it sure is snow. I think they might be planning it right now. Kenji's pretty cool. I'd like to see him again.

In fact, if we time it right, maybe he could accompany Father, Linda (Father's S.O. - significant other), Rudy and me to Florida next month.

Father has some dealings down there with a resort corporation based in Orlando, right near, well, you know.

The big place with the castle and the mouse! I hear there are lots of real animals to see too, like manatees and sea turtles in wildlife preservation areas.

Anyway, I guess this is where I say thanks again for tuning in and reading my travel diary. Don't forget to check me out on the web.* I'll let you know what happens on my next trip. Let's make it a date!

C ya!
K.C.

*http://www.rdppub/KookCase

Here is an excerpt from the second novel
in the **K.C. Flanagan, girl detective** series,

CHAOS IN CANCÚN.

I crept closer to the edge of the cliff, reaching for my binoculars and peering down in fascination. What appeared to be an orange buoy bobbed violently atop the waves below me, a marker for what I couldn't imagine.

"Careful," Julian said, as he grabbed my arm and pulled me gently back from the edge of the cliff. "The wind can be pretty strong at this height. You don't want it to take you by surprise up here." His blue eyes were friendly and frank.

"I saw something down there," I told him as he released my arm.

"Oh?" he said, his dark brows arching upward in surprise. "What?" I shook my head, frowning.

"I couldn't quite make it out, but there seemed to be an orange buoy down there, by the cliffs."

"That's not possible," he told me gently. "Those rocks are off limits, they're far too dangerous for people to approach and no reason for a buoy. It must have been a piece of flotsam." Rudy had strolled over to join us in time to catch Julian's remark.

"Seeing things again, Kook Case?" he asked me, offering a commiserating smile to Julian. "Don't mind my little sister, Julian. She's got an overactive imagination."

"I do not!" I protested.

"We all have our little idiosyncrasies," Julian commented obliquely and, giving me a crooked sideways smile took my arm gently once more, steering me further away from the edge of the cliff. I thought that my little spat with Rudy had gone unnoticed, but then I saw Linda eyeing both of us thoughtfully.

"How about if Rudy and your father drive back to the hotel in one cart and you and Julian and I take the other cart? I'd love to hear about your day, honey," Linda suggested. Julian and I exchanged friendly glances.

"It's all right with me," I agreed.

"No problem," Julian said, and handed her the keys to the cart. "Is it all right if you drive, Linda? I have a few notes to make on our progress today."

"Oh, but I might want to take pictures or write things down," Linda replied, holding the keys out to me. "How about you. K.C., you up for driving?"

"Sure," I smiled, happily accepting the keys.

Julian took the passenger seat and Linda sat behind me as I started the cart. The little engine sputtered to life, noisy but not noisy enough to prohibit conversation.

Julian pulled a small black notebook out of his shirt pocket and jotted something in it as I guided the cart along the road back to Isla Mujeres, following Rudy and Father. After he finished writing he turned to Linda and me with a smile.

"So, how do you like Isla Mujeres?"

"It's paradise," I told him quite sincerely, "glorious and quiet." In fact, the island was about as relaxed a place as anywhere I'd ever been.

Not that I was complaining, mind you. My last 'vacation' with Rudy and Father several months ago in Puerto Vallarta had turned into a "bang-bang" adventure as I'd tangled with a nasty drug smuggler. As far as I was concerned, peace and quiet were far preferable to that kind of action any day.

"Not much happens here," Julian shrugged. "It's not a big center of commerce or anything. The main industries here are tourism and fishing." I nodded. The small town of Isla Mujeres was popular as a jumping-off point for tourists heading out to Cancún, Cozumel and Chichén Itzá.

"What does Isla Mujeres mean, anyway?" I asked Julian curiously.

"It means Isle of Women," he told me, "the Spanish conquistadors named it when they first came to the Yucatán Peninsula in 1517."

"Why? People say it's because this is where the Spanish buccaneers used to keep their women, um —" she stopped in mid-sentence, and out of the corner of my eye I saw her glance at me.

"Mistresses?" I supplied the missing word and Linda shrugged, then nodded.

"Well, captives, prisoners of war, ladies, you know," she finished somewhat lamely, obviously deeming a more colorful description to be unsuitable for one of my tender years.

"Spanish buccaneers huh?" I repeated. "You mean, as in pirates?" There was a short pause and then Julian answered me.

"This island is famous for having once been a stopping point for Spanish slave traders and pirates, yes."

"The entire Yucatán coast was frequented by merchants and pirates in the mid 1500's, wasn't it?" Linda asked and Julian nodded in response.

I concentrated on driving while Julian and Linda talked about the history of the Spanish invasion of Mexico.

In 1517 Francisco Hernandez de Cordova was the first official Spaniard to see the 'New World,' as South America was considered by Europeans. His discovery was followed by increasing interest from Spain, which in 1519 sent Hernan Cortès to buy Mayan slaves.

Eight years after that Francisco Montejo and his son had traveled inland, taking the Yucatán by force.

The Spanish conquest of the Mayan people was aided by the diseases the Spaniards had brought with them. Huge numbers of the Mayan people were believed to have been wiped out by smallpox, chicken pox and influenza, making the conquest a simple matter of medical fact.

"Like the black plague," Linda commented, taking notes as Julian went on.

"About that devastating to the Mayan population, yes," Julian confirmed.

We were more than halfway back to the town of Isla Mujeres and were passing what looked like a private airstrip on our right side. I wanted to study it along with the fairly posh neighborhood surrounding it more closely, but traffic was picking up now so I stayed alert.

"What were the Mayas like?" I asked, "before the Spanish came, I mean." I'd done a little reading on the subject myself but was still interested in hearing his opinion.

"Have you been to see any of the nearby Mayan ruins yet?" he answered my question with one of his own and I shook my head.

"No, why?"

"It would be easier to explain them if you had." He looked over his shoulder at Linda and asked, "Why don't we all go see Chichén Itzá together tomorrow? Are you free?" Linda's face lit up.

"Really?" She was obviously trying not to gush. "That would be great, Julian. I'll have to talk to James about it but as far as this article is concerned it would be best if I could interview you right at the location of your discovery."

"Discovery?" I repeated curiously. Linda leaned forward to explain:

"Julian was restoring part of the ancient city of Chichén Itzá and he discovered a stone calendar indicating the beginning of Mayan time. It is one of the most significant archaeological discoveries in recent years, K.C."

"Wow," I said, deeply impressed. Julian shot me a bemused glance.

"One of the calendars used by the ancient Mayas is called the long count and dates back to 3114 B.C.," Julian explained. "We don't know why they chose that date, but it was very significant to them for some reason."

We were approaching the outskirts of the town of Isla Mujeres and driving required all of my concentration so I stopped talking. I was sharing the road with a chaotic jumble of pedestrians, sunburned tourists in swimsuits, mopeds, taxis and other golf carts.

If we had been somewhere else in the world, in Florida for example, the chaos would have been annoying, but this was Isla Mujeres; here it was cool, people were relaxed and in no particular hurry. Instead of the impatience which is common in congested areas there were smiles as each one waited courteously for the other to pass or turn in a display of civility too often absent from Norh American city driving.

I turned right at Matamoros and drove three blocks to the hotel Vista Del Mar. It was an easy building to spot from a distance, owing mostly to the fact that it was painted a deep aqua color, with dusky pink and purple balconies wrapped around the open front of the building.

Many of the buildings on Isla Mujeres were ultra-colorful and had brightly patterned awnings which served to shade the narrow sidewalks below and the pedestrians there. Still, a lot of people strolled along right in the middle of the street, making it a real challenge for me to maneuver the golf cart safely among them.

When we reached the hotel I turned into the small courtyard in back and parked there. Luiz, the man at the reception desk, took the keys from me with a smile. Father and Rudy were already inside the hotel, waiting for us in the lobby.

"Meet for dinner later?" Julian directed the question at Linda and after a quick glance at my father who nodded, Linda replied:

"Sure, the buffet is at eight." Julian nodded, collected his mail and headed upstairs to the apartment he and the other members of his crew were sharing.

"Well," Father said as we took the stairs up to our own apartment. "What do you think?"

"It's hot," Rudy replied fervently, fanning himself with a magazine.

"He's nice," Linda replied.

"About what?" I asked. Father led us down a long, mauve hallway with a pink tiled floor toward a narrow stairway arching up.

"About Isla Mujeres," Father clarified, unlocking the door which led to our apartment. We were staying for a whole week and so, instead of renting single rooms, Father and Linda had decided to take advantage of the fact that the Hotel Vista Del Mar also offered spacious family apartments for short term rent.

"The island is cool," I answered, following Rudy inside the foyer. The living room was quite large, and very colorful. The walls were pale aqua, the floor was tiled in deep blue-green, and most of the wooden furniture had been painted in black enamel. The instant he'd seen it Rudy had developed a fixation about the centerpiece of the room, a puffy purple sofa embroidered with a flamboyant red floral pattern.

"So, was Julian how you expected him to be?" Father asked Linda with curiousity as she tossed her straw hat on the hat stand and headed for the kitchen. Rudy sat gingerly on the sofa, eyeing it briefly as though uncertain if it were friend or foe, then switched on the TV.

"Not really," Linda replied from the kitchen, where she got a bottle of iced tea from the refrigerator, "although I guess I'd expected him to be a little more stuffy than he is. Anyone else want some tea?"

"Me," I answered quickly. The tropical sun made me thirsty.

"I'd like one," Father added.

"Me too," Rudy spoke up and Linda returned a moment later, bearing chilled bottles of iced tea which she handed around.

I waited until everyone had had a minute to sip their tea, then announced: "Julian had a great idea for tomorrow."

Father quirked an eyebrow at me. "What's that?"

"It's about Chichén Itzá," Linda explained. "He suggested that we go to the ruins tomorrow, and offered to give us a tour of the site."

"Sounds like a good idea. What do you think, Rudy?" Father asked, raising an eyebrow in his best Irish manner.

"Fine with me," Rudy answered.

"Let's do it then," Father said. Linda's grin lit up the room.

"Oh, James," she went to give him a big hug, burying her face in his chest, "you're such a doll." He gave her a tender smile and they kissed, right in front of us! It can be a little disconcerting the way they carry on like that, I mean, they've been dating for two years but they still act like smitten teenagers.

Rudy and I never really talked about it but I think we both assume they will get married someday, although they don't seem to be in any big hurry to formally tie the knot. Linda has her own apartment in Montreal, where she lives when she's not traveling on business and Father enjoys his independence too. For now, they seem pretty happy with the way things are.

Tactfully, Rudy and I strolled out and up onto the paved rooftop of the hotel, an open expanse which stretched along one side of our apartment like a private garden. There was a fountain up there, three large potted palms and several wicker chairs in a cluster near a round wooden picnic table.

Rudy and I stood there in silence, watching as the sun set over the sea, the blue-green sky deepening into midnight blue over the velvet water which washed in gentle waves onto the white sand. Five little boys were playing soccer in a circle on the beach, kicking the ball back and forth and laughing when the ball rolled close to the waves.

"I wonder what she's doing right now," Rudy murmured, his eyes on the soccer game, his thoughts obviously elsewhere.

"Pamela," I said with resignation. It was the only word which could get through to Rudy.

"She's great, isn't she." He said it with such conviction that I knew contradicting him would only result in serious discord. I just nodded, sinking into one of the wicker chairs, and as if on cue, Rudy took the chair opposite me and leaned forward with an earnest look.

"What if she meets someone else while I'm here?" he asked, and I shook my head gently, trying hard not to be impatient with him. I would have been more sympathetic toward Rudy, but this had been going on for a month and it was getting a little stale.

"Then she isn't right for you," I replied simply. Rudy's worried look increased slightly so I pointed out reasonably, "Look, Rudy, we'll only be here for a week. Then we'll head home and everything will be fine." His face brightened then sank.

"A lot can happen in a week," he sighed heavily, his shoulders slumping. Patiently, I decided to try another approach.

"Look, Rudy, you're a cool guy, what girl could possibly forget you in one week?" A small smile crossed his face.

"That's true," he admitted self-consciously. The sound of laughter drew our attention back to the room where Father and Linda were seated side by side on the sofa, laughing together at something she had just said.

"They're so happy," Rudy's wistful look returned. "I wish Pamela were here now."

"Well she's not, so snap out of it, all right?" My small reserve of sibling understanding was gone and Rudy turned a look of hurt surprise on me at my harsh words. I sighed, "I'm sorry Rudy, it's just that you've been going on and on about Pamela for weeks now and —." Rudy held up a hand, deeply injured.

"Never mind K.C. I can see you're just too young to understand." He left me with pained dignity, heading for his own room, and I watched him go with mingled pity and frustration.

It wasn't like Rudy to mope, but he was definitely moping. I was starting to feel a little worried about him but I really couldn't think of anything to do to help him snap out of it. And after his response to my latest advice I had to admit that tough love wasn't the best way to go.

I got up and wandered downstairs, strolling one block toward the deserted end of the north beach. For a while I stood and watched the waves roll in and then I noticed a large white yacht docked at one of two long concrete piers stretching out from shore. I contemplated it curiously.

I was pretty sure the yacht hadn't been there earlier in the day, I knew I would have remembered seeing it if it had been. I studied the big vessel closely, she was about seventy-five feet long, enameled white with gold trim. There might have been the gleam of a satellite dish on the top deck. I walked closer, intrigued.

A movement caught my eye and as I watched, a short, husky man in a white suit and panama hat strode into view. He paced across the deck to stand at the side of the railing, looking expectantly toward shore as though waiting for someone. He didn't notice me standing there, but something about him made me feel uneasy. Without even knowing why I shivered as I watched him turn away abruptly, his attention caught by a second man I now saw walking down the length of the pier to board the yacht.

The first man, the one in white, now had his back to me as he stood on deck talking to the newcomer who was wearing faded blue jeans and a nondescript soiled white work shirt. I could see his face and studied it closely.

He looked like he was about thirty-five years old or so, with thick blond hair cut stylishly short and a handsome, rugged face. As I watched, the man in white reached into his breast pocket and pulled out a fat manila envelope. I caught the glint of gold on an unusual pinky ring the man in white was wearing and frowned, wondering where I had seen that ring before. I took another step toward the pier, watching as the second man took the envelope and lifted the flap. He peered inside with a twisted smile, then glanced around furtively and stuffed the envelope hastily into the pocket of his pants. He left quickly without any goodbyes, hurrying back the way he'd come. The man in white turned to watch his progress, looking straight at me, and I gasped as he turned enough for me to get a clear look at his face.

It was a face I recognized from my recent experiences on the other side of Mexico, in the Pacific coast resort town of Puerto Vallarta, and although I had only seen its owner briefly, it was a face I would never forget. The man was Señor Hernan Colón, a notoriously corrupt member of the Mexican government who had been indicted on charges of protecting a ring of drug smugglers in Puerto Vallarta. He had fled Mexico for Ireland and then to Canada after his nefarious activities had been uncovered, but was extradited back to Mexico to face charges after I recognized him in Montreal.

Since I was one of the people who had been instrumental in bringing him to justice, you can imagine the shock of fear I felt at seeing him here on Isla Mujeres, when he was supposed to be in jail pending trial.

For a split second we stared at each other, mutual recognition crackling between us like a current of electricity, then Señor Colón shouted something unintelligible and pointed at me, his face contorting with rage as yet another man appeared from the inside of the yacht's cabin.

I watched in horror as the third man listened to Colón's shouted instructions then turned and sprinted toward the pier, heading in my direction. It was clear he was coming for me and although I had no way of knowing what his intentions were I had a definite feeling that he didn't mean to engage me in a simple chat about the weather.

I took off, running as fast as I could toward the concrete promenade ahead of me through thick white sand which slowed me despite my best efforts at speed. After about fifty yards I glanced over my shoulder, hoping that I had lost my pursuer, but he was hot on my trail, in fact he was gaining on me.

Sheer terror lent wings to my feet and when I reached the concrete promenade I sprinted through the small crowd of people gathered there to view the sunset, ignoring their stares as I headed for the safety of the jumble of houses about one hundred yards away.

From the commotion behind me it was evident that I was still being pursued so I didn't waste time looking over my shoulder but turned down a small side street, weaving in and out of the vendors' stalls, past rows of colorful hand-painted masks and ceramics. At some other time I might have paused to admire the art but I could hear the slap of my pursuer's feet on the cobblestones as he came after me through the crowd.

Despite the safety my hotel represented, I knew it would be foolish for me to head straight back there, since the last thing I wanted was for Señor Colón to know where I was staying (We were registered at the hotel under Linda's name, so Colón wouldn't be able to trace me directly).

I turned two corners in rapid succession and darted into the secluded courtyard of a private residence where I crouched behind a potted palm, watching for the seconds it took my pursuer to sprint past my hiding place and disappear down the street.

After I was sure he was gone I stood up shakily and looked around at the stupefied stares of an elderly couple who had evidently been sitting down to dinner in the quiet privacy of their own home before being rudely interrupted by my intrusion.

"Um, *lo siento, señora, señor,*" I shrugged and spread my hands, indicating that it had all been a mistake and that I was sorry to have disturbed them. "I'm sorry, please forgive me." The elderly man at the table exchanged puzzled glances with his wife who turned to me with a cool shrug, motioning away the impolite *gringa.* "I'll just be on my way now," I added apologetically, skulking back into the street.

I walked quickly back to the hotel Vista Del Mar, peering around myself every few steps for fear that I might again encounter Colón's henchman. The scariest part of the whole thing was wondering what Señor Colón was doing on Isla Mujeres in the first place, when he was supposed to be safely locked up in Mexico City.

That he had recognized me as I had recognized him was undeniable and it seemed clear from his reaction that he was not at all happy with my presence on the island. Dejectedly, I turned into the stairs leading to the veranda of the hotel, casting one last look over my shoulder to be certain I was unobserved before heading upstairs to tell Father what I had seen. I found him on the roof, looking for me.

Achevé d'imprimer
sur les presses de l'Imprimerie Quebecor,
L'Éclaireur, Beauceville